A Good Place on the Banks of the Euphrates

stories from the war against ISIS

Warren Stoddard II

PINE NEEDLE FLOOR
Birmingham, Alabama

ISBN: 978-0-578-96484-3

Cover design by Nick Resty
Original artwork: *Homenaje a las Brigadas Internacionales*
by José Bardasano

Map (page 7) by Warren Stoddard II

Contents

An Introduction by the Author

I count myself very fortunate to have played some small part in an incredibly special time and place in the history of the world. I am only one of many. Estimates vary widely, but somewhere between 300 and 3,000 international volunteers traveled to Northeastern Syria between 2015 and 2019 to join the YPG and YPJ. We were welcomed with open arms by Kurdish friends we met there. We have been called many things since then: brave, stupid, selfless, selfish. We have been accused of harboring death wishes and of war-tourism, of petty theft and terrorism. We've had bounties placed on our heads (my own amounted to more money than every dollar I've ever made in my life), and we've been portrayed as little more than emotionally empty, glory-seeking Hemingway-heroes.

For the record, I did carry a copy of *For Whom the Bell Tolls* with me in my backpack when I crossed the border into Syria.

Without Hemingway's portrayal of American volunteer Robert Jordan's sacrifice as a member of the International Brigades in the Spanish Civil War 80 years prior, many of us likely would not have ever found our way to Rojava. The International Brigades in Spain paved the way for us all. They stood there as historical precedent saying "Yes, in fact, you *can* do this." There is nothing stopping you but imaginary lines on made-up maps that have come to serve as the basis for every horrible crime of inaction.

They are not our people, so why should we care?

But they are. The Kurds are a beautiful people, and their civilization—one of the oldest in the world—the place where the wheel was invented, agriculture, and many other things we have come to regard as pieces of the bedrock of civilization, is in every way as valuable as America and its land of strip malls (it may be difficult to believe, but yes, this is something you *actually* have to convince people of).

This is not to say that the time I spent in Syria was one without frustration, anger, or immense longing for home and the comforts of a Mexican restaurant. Much of my time there was spent just so; when I go back and read them, many of my journal entries are bitter and angry at inaction—inherently ignorant of the place I was and unappreciative of the time I had with the society I found myself in. I regret that I ever felt that way when I look back at the war and the Revolution now. There was never anything more beautiful.

But when at last I was at the front line, I could have done it forever. It is a strange thing to say, but in that serene place of duty and purpose and glory and horrific awfulness I was home. It was what I had wanted for my whole life to do. It was the right thing to do, to fight for, and had it not been for the things that unfolded, I would have never left Rojava until the only rounds fired were those of celebration at the defeat of ISIS. But life rarely works out how we wish, does it?

So much has been written about war that it seems redundant to write about yet another human conflict, but it continues to enthrall both those taking part and those who do not. As Anthony Swofford said in *Jarhead*: "Every war is different. Every war is the same." And in Syria this held no less true, but *something* was different about this conflict. It was perhaps the first war in the history of the world which curious civilians on the other side of the planet could follow in live time, house by house. There was and is at the time of my writing this an endless stream of news coming out of Syria. It is the most reported-on war in the history of wars. Period. The internet and social media have taken war-reporting to new heights in this modern age, and anyone who wants to find the information can. That is how all of us got our start headed there.

The action many of us took in going on our own to Rojava should not be confused as a proclamation of the great white savior coming to rescue the Kurds from the brink of extinction. They simply would have done it whether we had been there or not. Forty-five internationals were killed in the course of the war out of over 11,000 members of the multiracial, Kurdish-led SDF. They didn't *need* us, but to many of those I spoke to, our very being there brought them the glimmer of hope needed to believe that the outside world was taking note of what was happening in Syria at the time, and that the people of the world cared what became of the people in Syria, whether our home nations truly did or not. So when we came to fight, we came as representatives unsanctioned by our own governments, willing to show to these people and everyone else that the world is perhaps still "a fine place and worth the fighting for," as Hemingway famously said in *For Whom the Bell Tolls,* that there is light in an otherwise unending and overwhelming dark. We hope our sacrifice was worthwhile. We hope the sacrifice of the Kurds and Arabs and Yazidis and Syriacs was one-hundred-fold. Of course, every sacrifice ever made in similar circumstances held the same hope.

The first war in recorded history was fought 4,700 years ago in ancient Mesopotamia. Since then, men have been caught in the repetition of wars like a pirouette. Reliving them. Revisiting them. Acting them out. Blending fact and mythical precedent. Singing songs. And in the days and years that follow your war, you relive it one hundred times. You turn left instead of right. You fall where you once stood, so that you fight ten thousand wars before you die, only ever having fought one—every war different. But every war is the same. And they have written books on all of them, from Caesar to Salah ad-Din to Napoleon to Ho Chi Minh. This was our war, fought in a good place on the banks of the Euphrates and told here through fiction, nonfiction, and scrawled journal entries written in the prelude to, in the heat of, and in the aftermath of it all—then reliving it again and again—forever.

Sîlav û rezên şoreşgerî,
Heval Azad Pinkling

"However much one cursed at the time, one realized afterwards that one had been in contact with something strange and valuable."

-George Orwell: *Homage to Catalonia*

"Give a Kurd a pack of cigarettes and a Kalashnikov, stand him on top of the mountain, and send the whole world."

-Kurdish proverb

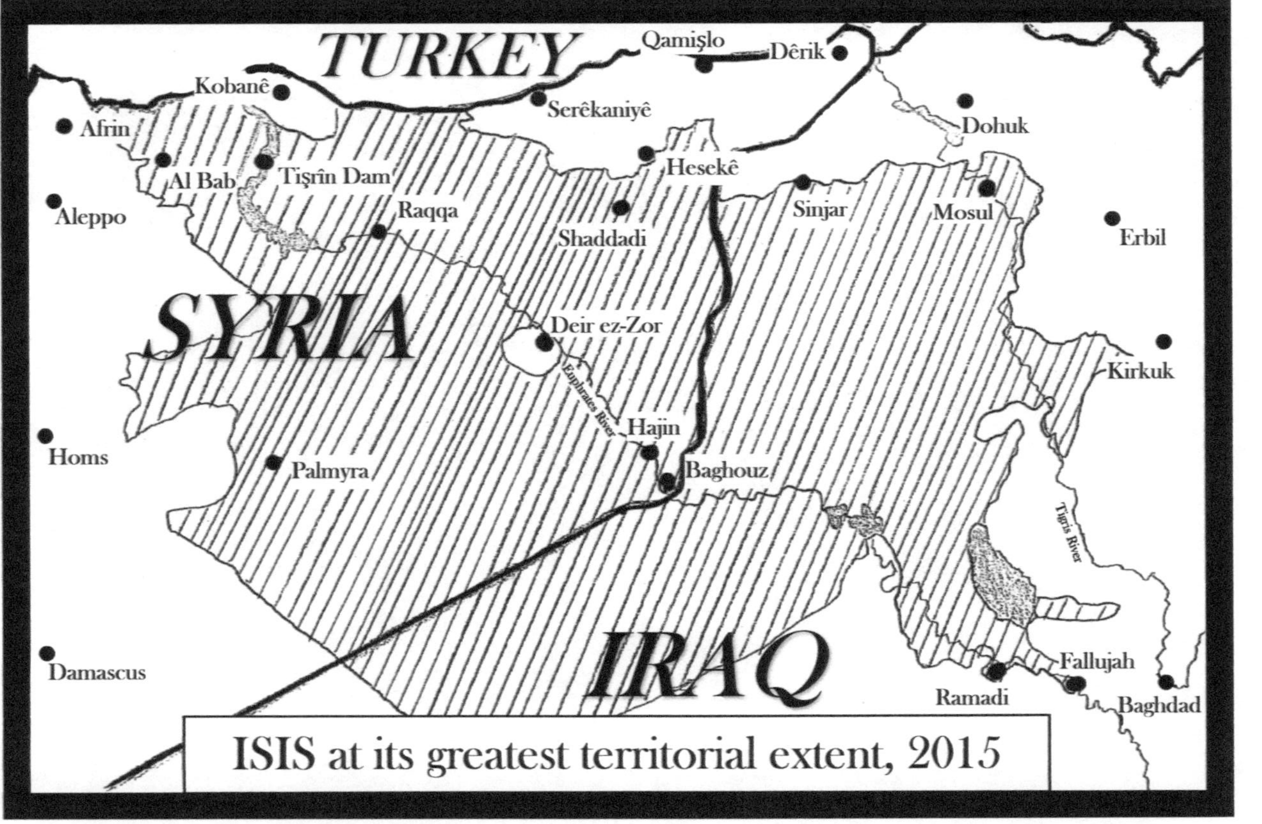

ISIS at its greatest territorial extent, 2015

Warren Stoddard II

Ghanima

In the night you had an awful lot of time to yourself to wonder what in the hell you were really doing there. And so he did. The room was garishly lit by an upturned flashlight. Its beam, reflecting off the dusty ceiling, lit men in haphazardly arranged and mismatching uniforms. The only similarities they had were the small, yellow, shield-shaped patches on their shoulders that read YPG.

The People's Protection Units, he thought, Yekinêya Parastîna Gel. Had he done so much protecting? Could killing of any sort be any kind of protection? *Killing*?

The sun's final dying embers lingered stoically on the horizon through the window. In the distance he heard the rattle of a Biksî–the PKM machine gun–sounding out to remind them all that there was a war to be won. "Another one bites the dust," he said. Somewhere in another corner of the room another heval grunted an affirmative reply. He reached his arm out from under the blanket and grabbed his Kalashnikov, pulling it into the warmth of the little mattress with him. Feeling the steel of the rifle against his abdomen.

It was hard to remember the war was there when you were not in it. In the evenings and in the days you slept or ate or read a book among falling mortar shells. It is not that it went unnoticed. The war permeated everything–the walls of the buildings were shattered, jets laced the sky with potent venom, your rifle always remained within arm's reach, a round in the chamber. War had just seemed such a novel and interesting thing when read about, when acted out with army men, when experienced through a television screen. Hell, he had traveled from a comfortable life in America to a place halfway around the world to see it–to fight it–for no money. All humanity loved to glorify war, dramatize it. In truth it was little more than waiting, watching a window, and a distinct few brief moments of absolute panic.

Is there any intrinsic value in any of this? he asked himself. When I am old and I am gray and I can say to my grandchild, "Let me tell you about the war..." was that the value of it? The *ghanima*? The spoils of war. To one day add your name to humanity's all-important registry of waiters–warfighters–heroic, noble?

What a fucking stupid proposition, he said to himself. He hoped he believed himself, but he knew otherwise.

I needed to be here, he told himself. He stood from the thin mattress and folded the blanket neatly atop it. Wrapping his shoulders in the floral black scarf so emblematic of his chosen cause, he made for the stairwell of the building with his rifle held by the crook of the magazine in his hand. It was time for *nobet*–guard duty.

On the rooftop, the sentry was staring idly over the ruined city.

"Hîwa?" the sentry asked as he heard footsteps behind him.

"Yeah."

Hîwa stood beside him, gazing over a heavy blackness so still that your eyes could not handle it. They created static, made the silhouettes of buildings waver against the sky; the ground shimmered, the stars shifted, convincing you there was something out there.

"I think we've won," the sentry said, speaking with a French inflection in his voice.

Hîwa adjusted his beanie on his head and slung his rifle lightly over one shoulder. He held it by the pistol grip casually. "Did we?" he asked.

"I think so. No movement, not anything. All the shots are coming from our side." The sentry unclipped a radio from his vest and handed it to Hîwa. "Don't get killed," he said.

It would be hard to imagine it, after all this, but then it always is. To have fought and killed and bled and felt the blood of your friends hot on your arm, the winds cold in the night, and the sun hot in the days before the rains came, and with autumn the seemingly unending downpour—day after day. Until it ended. The sun came out, the fields turned green, it became cold, and that was the end of it. It would be hard too to imagine spring after so long a winter.

He wondered if they knew they would die. In those brief moments of panic, in the sights of his rifle, or in the scope of the Dragunov, they had gone about their business—whether shooting at his friends or squatting in the shade. He didn't feel bad about it. He didn't feel anything about it, and in some ways that was worse than the feeling bad. Utter contempt—a sneer—they got what was coming to them—of what importance is any life like that?

He had seen all the videos. Everyone had. *ISIS*. The beheadings. The flames. The black flag waving and murdering with bastardized benediction. A whole beautiful corner of this world decimated for words in a book, *for nothing*. Only a few hundred meters away they had led out those who resisted and decapitated and decollated the detractors in the Al-Naim Traffic Circle. Those unfortunate enough to live silent under their scourge, peddling their wares from city to city, saw the bodies of nonbelievers and dissidents up for display the very first instant their vehicles entered Raqqa. Bodies left to fester, to be eaten by the crows. For years the survivors quietly seethed, watching their friends and family rot in the sun. And now they had exacted their revenge.

He supposed there was no good reason for a war, but this must have been pretty damned close.

And now it was all rubble. Airstrikes, mortars, heat, wind, bullets, and hate had whittled this de-facto capital to nothing. The walls were in shambles, the shops' roofs caved in, oranges rolled out into the dusty street. You could smell the citrus—even among the stench of decaying bodies. So many dead, he thought. Was that what he had come for? To kill? To understand what it is to handle life as a god might?

In those moments of panic you fired your weapon and they stopped firing back. They stumbled into safety. They fell face-first into the street. You fired and they stopped fighting. You never saw them, but you saw their panicked faces and the frantic prayers of their friends. And then you fired again. And you fired again. And you fired again. And again. And again.

Until it was nothing to you. Until you were one with the war. Until you had fought it. Until you had won.

In the morning, victory was declared. The YPG, YPJ, and SDF forces entered the stadium, that last stronghold. And ISIS was defeated in Raqqa, their capital now somewhere else surely, but not here, and though the war to eradicate them would rage on for nearly two more years, victory was all that mattered today.

Around the tattered stadium, uniformed Arabs and Kurds and Syriacs and white-skinned foreign volunteers took selfies with their smart phones, fired celebratory bursts of automatic rifle fire into the air, and posed for group photos with their loot: black ISIS flags, gold coins, swords stained pink in their grooves, antiquated bolt-action and black-powder rifles engraved in Arabic.

"I've got to get me one of those," Hîwa said.

"A flag?" the Frenchman asked, gesturing to one as men held it up for a picture. "What use have you for a flag? The flag of Daesh?"

"I've just got to have it."

"Will you fly it?"

"No."

"Then what use have you for the flag of Daesh?"

He could not explain it. Trying to rationalize it was like trying to rationalize this whole endeavor. Why would a man leave his comfortable home in America to come to Rojava, to war-torn Syria and fight against terrorists he had never suffered under and for the revolution of the people of a land he had never seen? Why would he want to take home the flag of the enemy he had killed and who themselves had killed hundreds of thousands of people, and fold and tuck the scrap of cloth away in a box only to be brought out when he wished to delve into nostalgia or impress descendants in some far-off and unpromised future? He could not say, he only knew that he had to have one. He had to have the black flag of terror that he himself tore down from the city walls it once beamed so proudly over. He had helped take the city. He would take a flag too.

"It is just a stupid piece of cloth," the Frenchman said, and he rolled his eyes and sighed and acquiesced and said, "Let us go find you one."

They left the stadium in a hurry, avoiding the watchful eyes of commanders. Outside, the once-motionless streets began to twitter with the first signs of life since the battle had begun months prior. YPG fighters walked openly in the streets, their Hilux pickups parked along the curb. *Sabotaj* units patrolled the city, scanning through buildings for unexploded ordinance, disarming them, piling IEDs up outside the doorways of the high-rise apartments of Raqqa.

The pair walked openly, but their eyes were alert, darting from alleyways and ledges where ISIS fighters had once emerged. Placid sun shone. They could hear the rattle of celebratory machinegun fire. They could smell the citrus in the shops and the bodies decaying above them. Their scarves were dusty, and they had walked a long way.

"Here looks good," Hîwa said, his voice growing weary—months of fighting, of being shelled, of auditory fatigue finally began to set in. He felt his nerves release, his mind relaxed, now unafraid of impending death—the ease of life could resume—desires be felt. "I'm hungry, anyway."

"I hope there will be *şawarma* and a fire tonight," the Frenchman said, unslinging his rifle from his shoulder as he entered.

"And dancing," Hîwa hoped.

The building was another of Raqqa's many high-rise apartments, shooting up some ten stories. The tentative burbling of peace had not yet reached through the door. The inside was still shrouded in the uneasy silence of war. Blankets were strewn about haphazardly. Ceilings hung like broken bat's wings. Shell casings littered the floor, tinkling sweetly beneath their feet as they walked—brass windchimes.

"It is... something in here," the Frenchman said, "I cannot think of the word."

"Spooky? Unnerving?"

"Yes. Unnerving. It is a good word."

Hîwa held his rifle low but ready, the Frenchman the same, they both slid off the safeties of the AKs as quietly as they could allow and ascended the first flight of stairs, scanning the floor for tripwires, carefully stepping over things that could be booby trapped—tea kettles, heaters, blankets—those comforts most immediately desired in the discomfort of war.

Their minds again began to race, now the hopes of the evening were gone, replaced instead by survival instinct, but the cognitive dissonance of their objective was not lost on them.

"Are you sure this flag is worth it?" the Frenchman asked as they mounted the second set of stairs.

"We'll be fine," Hîwa responded. "We'll be fine."

They checked each room as they passed, rifle barrels entering first, followed by quick darts of the head before finally stepping under the lintel. Each one empty. Bare walls, all pockmarked by bullet holes. Shell casings.

The third and fourth sets of stairs passed under their feet. On the fifth floor Hîwa darted his head into a room and found it empty. He stepped through casually and out onto a small patio overlooking the all but destroyed city of Raqqa. "I wonder what it was like before all this," he called to the Frenchman behind him.

"You've arrived a bit late to see that, haven't you?"

He had. "But I arrived in time to see all of this. They'll be talking about us forever, you know." The sky was clear and brilliantly blue. The wind skirled across the ruins.

"Yes, Achilles, they will. But you know what they say, heval. 'Şehîd na mirin.' Our martyrs never die. They will have their faces still up on posters long after you and I have gone home and told everyone we know of what we did here, and we and they have all died. We'll be forgotten as quickly as winter. Our friends, those who fell, will live forever."

Out of the corner of his eye, Hîwa saw something–a rag, a scrap of cloth fleetingly fluttering. Black, in the room next door, pulled by the wind out an open window. He broke into a smile. "Oh, heval. We have got it. You can keep all the copper Daesh coins you like. And I will take my 'scrap of cloth'."

"You have found one? Where?"

"Just over here," he said.

And he stepped into the room nonchalantly, as a conqueror might. As Caesar might have strode across the Forum. He had come. He had seen the plight of these people, so tortured by the Islamic State. He had fought the war. And he had taken their capital. Their flag would come with him. Never to flutter again in the breeze of the plains of Syria. He would tuck it in some box somewhere, taking it out only when he sought to bathe in euphoric nostalgia, wincing as long-ago bullets whizzed past, ever feeling the panic and the recoil of his rifle and feeling the dust, kicked up by the winds, settling in his eyes.

The flag was hung by nails driven into the concrete wall. They settled loosely in their cavities. He pulled the first one out with ease, regarding it with contempt and speaking over his shoulder to the Frenchman as he flung the nail out the open window. "I knew all this wouldn't be so difficult."

The Frenchman was leaning casually against the frame of the door, arms crossed, and his eyes widened.

Hîwa had some difficulty pulling the second nail out, but after a few determined wiggles he broke it free, the black flag, the divine scrap of cloth now his. And somewhere just behind him, very faintly, as though through a change in the air in the room, he felt the perception of a soft click and a wave of violent heat. He did not hear it. He felt it coming, as one feels the seasons begin to change from far away. And slowly that interval rolls toward you until spring has come. Autumn has fell. Very briefly–instantaneously it came to him from across the room. And that was the end of it.

28 June 2018: The Academy, Rojava:

"In every part of the world they have different bacteria, & in the Middle East our bacteria is as strong as our dictators." - A mustachioed commander, upon hearing that I was sick & needed to go to the hospital.

It was good to go into town, to eat in a restaurant, to have a connection with the outside world. I feel human again. Noelle seems to be enjoying herself working at the dentist back home. I miss her. The power in our room now is intermittent. The air is stifling. It is fucking hot. But at least I am not shitting myself anymore after the medicine. In the evenings the air is cool & the sunset's last light lingers in the dust hanging on the horizon. It is scattered by the dust, like a hazy prism. The full moon lifts itself slowly from beyond that line, rising between rusted iron electricity towers like a blood-red mammoth from a tar pit—tired, but doing what needs to be done, granting some perspective, a counterbalance to keep you grounded. You are not so very far away after all.

16 August 2018: The Academy, Rojava:

The party lived up to expectations. There was song & dance & sweet treats. Two girls that Agît & I made the crossing with were there—we danced together as old friends. As all friends are in Rojava. The left foot forward, the left foot back, the right foot forward, tap the heel, cross the left across the right, & again in a wide, pinky-linked spiral to the center. At the conclusion of the song there were exchanges of sweaty smiles, the wiping of brows, laughter, & showering applause. The celebration was in honor of Şehîd Agît—the first Kurdish guerrilla to fire a shot at the Turks in 1984. & the war has still not ended. Our return to the Academy came with the news of a Turkish airstrike in Şengal; ground blown apart hardly 100 miles from us. Nobet required alert ears, listening for the sound of planes, drones—searching to hear for that brief & terrifying few seconds of the sound of falling bombs before the world bursts at the seams with singing shrapnel & concussive heat that will send your existence unbearably white before making you bow to the darkness. But it is only the silence of the waiting & your ears deceiving you. You wait. In the dark the air hums—a figment of an imagination.

Warren Stoddard II

Into the Sun, Alone

The two were sitting under the awning of an outdoor café in the afternoon. The beer was cold. The waitress laid a platter of cold cheese and hot lamb sausages between them, and the sun slipped at an angle under the awning and shone bright amber on their shoes and ankles. They clinked glasses.

"Cheers, man," said one.

"It's good to see you again," said the other.

They sipped the beer and chatted like old friends as the sun slid lower in the sky. Their forks made quick work of the sausage and the cheese. They were smiling.

A lull came over the conversation and the two leaned back comfortably in their seats. The sun was in their laps now. The voices speaking Czech around them filled the air with a smooth white noise. The waitress brought a second round of beer and two shots of a clear Czech spirit.

"Here's to Prague!"

"To Praha," said the second as the glasses clinked together musically.

They both grimaced and sucked their teeth as the shot went down hot on the throat, and the pair fell to talking again—about old friends, places they'd been, women they'd been with, whether one would or would not sleep with the waitress, what beer they should order next, and then the topic the other would have liked to avoid.

"So what brings you to town, man?"

His voice caught in his throat, he looked down at the now sun-lit table as if the answers were inscribed in the wood or the stainless-steel appetizer plates or would rise from the residual foam in the empty beer mugs. The indecipherable voices echoed off the wall in a cacophony. The one finished his beer in a gulp as the waitress set a new pair of frothy mugs on the table.

The two raised the beers and heard the click and looked at each other over the tops of the mugs raised to their lips with unblinking eyes.

"Just passing through," the other said before taking a sip.

"The fuck is that supposed to mean?" the one asked and laughed to cut the tension. "Where are you headed?"

"Someplace."

"You don't know? On a world tour of one-way tickets?"

"Maybe."

"You can't tell me?"

"More along those lines, yeah," said the other. The sun was on their arms now.

Their conversation changed course; the one was moving soon—from Prague to Auckland. Going to make a regular Magellan out of himself, but without the dying, and with more booze, and with less money.

"Your girl going with you?"

"Hell, it was her idea."

They laughed and toasted to his good fortune. The sun was on their shoulders.

"When do you think you'll head back to Texas?" the other asked.

"When will you?"

The other was silent as he sipped his beer. The sun on him was hot and stained his armpits with sweat. He wiped froth from his mustache and pressed himself away from the table and firmly against the backrest of the bench. "I don't know," he said. And for the first time that day he was honest; the one could see the whites of his eyes the way you might see the honesty of a young fuzz-antlered buck in late November moments before it drops like a ton of bricks and wails with brief panic before the eyes go dull.

Now the sun was on their faces and they slid dark sunglasses over their eyes as the final round of beer was laid on the table and the mugs clinked together in cold silence under the heat of the afternoon sun.

"Jesus, man," said the first, "what the hell are you getting into?"

The other told him not to worry about it. He tugged at the chest of his shirt to cool himself and tried to explain in a roundabout fashion why it was that he might not be going home. He knew that as afternoon turned to night and as five drinks turned to ten the truth would spill out slurred and diminished by alcohol. It was best to keep it light for now. Then he reached in his bag and fished out an envelope with his friend's name scrawled on it. The one lifted the flap and began to pull out the folded papers inside.

THE LAST WILL AND TESTAMENT OF

He read this and his hand lingered for a moment as it might on a hot stove before the sting of the pain made its way to the brain. And then he jerked it away, tucked the papers back in the envelope and patted the package on the table with suspicion.

"I understand," he said.

They drank the beers while they were still cold and talked of rich fantasies as the heat of the sun subsided in the dying day.

The mugs were lined up, and the friends were smiling again when the checks came and were paid, and it was time to go. A thin bubble of Czech conversation kept the air from stilling.

"I know a good place just up the street a ways. Want to check it out?"

The other gathered his bag in his lap. "Yeah," he said. "I like this place though, it was nice."

The two stood from the table and left from under the awning and walked together down the street. "It's a nice place," the one said, "except for the sun."

16 September 2018: The Academy, Rojava:

"My favorite practical jokes are aubergine-related." - Dilsoz, after hiding an eggplant in the freezer.

Threw up my breakfast shortly after writing that. I do that a lot. Spent most of the morning miserable in bed. I do that a lot too, but it has always passed. That misery exists in sharp juxtaposition with the genuine heart-clenching joy I felt watching "The Americans" with the guys all gathered 'round the TV, or eating banana-yogurt-tea ice cream together, or staring with incredulity at NHK World's wild lineup of Japanese television. Got to talk to Noelle & Lopez for a bit on WhatsApp—Noelle about the general fun nothing that our conversations are, the kind that make you happy. With Lopez I talked about the chopper he wants me to help him build. Sometimes it feels like I exist in two worlds here. The one in present Rojava, the other in future Texas. I do not know if one detracts from the other or if it is beneficial to both my future & my present to have the mind constantly weighing them against each other. But it is good to have a mental escape from Alîşer's cooking—fucking burnt beans, again? & I feel that this constant subconscious contemplation of myself will help me get what it is that I truly want out of life. Whether Azad can be reconciled with Warren, if they can coexist, if the former is absorbed into the latter, or if one ceases to be remains to be seen. Time will tell. In any case, my near three mostly monotonous months here have indelibly changed who I am. So much waiting. So much of war is in the mind. The next 3 months promise to be much more action-packed, so to speak, & I wonder who I will be when they are complete.

Warren Stoddard II

A Return Home

When you walk into any hospital in America with a gunshot wound, you are bound to attract a lot of attention, bewildered looks, questions. "When did this happen?" Some weeks ago. "How many times were you shot?" Once, sort of. "Did they catch the guy who did it?" This final question proves to be the most difficult to answer, as in reality the man who squeezed the trigger of the DShK that fired the round which hit a wall and then you in many places is likely dead, blown to a million pieces, or captured–awaiting trial or deportation. "I was in Syria," you say, and even more heads in the room are turned towards you. It is like being a novice pianist at a water polo tournament. "What in the world were you doing there?"

Indeed, the first days back in the United States were experienced as one who has never seen electricity before experiences Las Vegas, and this hospital visit was no exception. I had spent the better part of the previous year in Kurdistan, predominantly North and Eastern Syria, as a member of YPG International, far from my homeland of Texas. Surely two sectors of the world must be more different, but if they exist, I have not seen them to make the comparison.

I left the State of Texas to journey halfway around the world to join the people of Northeastern Syria in the fight against the Islamic State. I transitioned abruptly from towering metropolises to windswept plains sporadically dotted with towns of stout cement structures, from the hectic, break-neck, dog-eat-dog pace of the United States of America to an incredibly leisurely tempo of life in Mesopotamia. I went knowing very little of what I would find in the Middle East. Of course, I had versed myself in the ideologies of the Syrian Democratic Forces and its Kurdish wing, the YPG—I knew well the ideals of feminism, direct democratic participation, ecology and grassroots socialism that were espoused by many of the texts I had pored over. But I also had to contend with a propagandized notion of fear instilled into most Americans at a young age about the people and the societies of the Middle East. "They'll kill you for your boots," I heard. "Those people just want another American to hold hostage and ransom," I was told. These statements could not have been farther from reality.

Immediately upon my arrival in Syria, I was greeted with a smile and a handshake. "Welcome to Rojava," the young Kurdish man said to me. I could see the white of his teeth bright in the darkness. "Come this way." And I was led into a world which I could hardly have imagined existed there in the arid lands that once were the Fertile Crescent. This society in the crossroads of the world—long plagued by outside influences and domineering nation-states—had adopted its own model of Utopia, and what is more impressive, they put it into action. From the ashes of the war against ISIS, these people had done it. Nearly everything that I had read in the required readings, the manifestos, and the writings of philosophical leaders of the Revolution had been implemented in the real world.

The countryside had long ago been stripped clean by passing empires—Phoenicians, Romans, Persians and Ottomans all played their part in the runaway deforestation that shaved the Middle East. Where once were lush oak groves were now plains in which little grew past a sapling before a passing flock of sheep nibbled the young plants for breakfast. This problem persisted for centuries. Oil derricks outnumbered tree trunks. No trees would grow because they simply could not get the time to do so before being consumed. It was nothing but rolling fields of wheat. The massive undertaking of reforesting Mesopotamia was largely laid by the wayside until recent years, when the people of this land set to animating those ideals long collecting dust in forgotten tomes. They began to plant. And it took little time at all for the effects to be noticed—there is a reason, after all, that they call this the Fertile Crescent. The soil between the Tigris and Euphrates is so rich in nutrients, the sun shines so brightly, and the rains fall so heavily in the wet season that the growth of any plant could be likened to a beanstalk. Now, where the rolling sunbaked plains once butted up to the periphery of villages, the passerby can rest in the bower, seeking shelter from the sun in pleasant copses of shade. Creek beds and river valleys exist as massive veins of green, carrying trees and water to the people and cities of the land.

Walking down the streets of those cities in Northeast Syria, an observer unfamiliar with the political framework of the region would be baffled at what they saw—women without headscarves in the Middle East? Churches next to mosques? Vendors selling produce that far outnumbered the amount of suicide bombers?

What we have been learned to accept as a stereotypical reality in Southwest Asia has been unilaterally shunned by the Syrian Democratic Council. Women lead many of the political wings in the region, making up more than the charter-mandated 40% of the government. Their children, Muslim or Christian, go to school side-by-side with those of different faiths. Arab children learn Kurdish as a second language; Kurdish children learn Arabic. And from the bottom of the society on up to the top, citizens are deeply involved in the political decision-making process—a democratic society situated in the heart of what one once considered to be a corner of the world reserved solely for oil-hoarding dictators.

And what's more, the people of this country*—of war-torn Syria* —are happy. Happy in the midst of the twenty-first century's bloodiest conflict. Before the Turkish invasion in October 2019, this corner of the country had been spared much of the unrest other regions have had to deal with in the previous decade, due in large part to its democratic mission. ISIS, as it was pushed back, territorial Caliphate shrinking ever more until it was nothing but a graveyard, left behind a long-suffering and war-weary populace yearning for peace and stability, yearning for a voice, and yearning for the right to pursue happiness however they saw fit. The result has been harmony edging on brotherhood between these constituents.

In the streets of the larger cities, shops' goods spill out of the stores' walls and onto the sidewalk—set up in a dazzling array of color and scent—oranges here, bananas there, spices, and baked goods. Competing shop owners wave hello and shake hands with one another as they roll up the doors to start the day. If one vendor does not have something, they will point you in the direction of one who may. Though they all sell many of the same goods, there is no single chain of businesses: no Walmart, or Target, or Walgreens, or anything of equal status as a corporation exists in Northeastern Syria, due both to the near-worldwide trade embargo imposed on the country and to its socialist leanings that drive to allow for the flourishing of small businesses.

It is needless to say that row upon row of McDonald's and Starbucks felt as foreign to me as not having a rifle in my hand when I returned to America nearly eight months later, now wounded, now carrying the good and the bad of this place with me. In a sense, I was not happy to be home—the America that I had grown up hearing heroic and noble tales of seemed to have fallen away in favor of an America dominated by corporate greed and asset interest—a country where instead of the will of the people, corporate lobbying controlled the actions of the government. The mere fact that thousands of Americans volunteered to fight against fascism in Spain in the 1930's—a civil war eerily similar to Syria's, and perhaps only a couple hundred made their way to the Levant in the 2010's despite vastly improved methods of transportation speaks volumes to this. To me, it felt that America had lost its way, that the US of A was no longer the obvious light in the dark that it had once been.

But what I considered the "American Dream" was alive and well in Rojava.

And in the hospital, flocked upon by bewildered medical personnel, home seemed a very lonely place. Who could understand any of this? There are very few. One nurse lifted his sleeve and showed me a scar. "Taliban sniper did this," he said, "So I get it." But did he? He understood the war, sure, the pain and the bloodshed and the screeching burning seething anger and everything terrible and addictive about the human urge to *fight,* but what he was fighting for were values won and defended hundreds of years prior–so far removed from present day motivations that they ought to be stored on a museum shelf and spoken of as one speaks of the merits of steel armor versus leather in regards to stopping arrows. The newness and tender vulnerability of revolution was gone from his fight, the desperate urge for success replaced with complacency and greed. Defend the oil.

A story: A Middle Eastern society seeks to establish a bastion of democracy between the Tigris and the Euphrates, and it is helped along by a world superpower until it becomes inconvenient for the superpower to do so. Money interests, nation-statism take over. Then the revolution is cast to the dogs, left to fend for itself in an arena stuffed with sharks and venomous snakes.

The revolution of Northeastern Syria was not so very different from our own in 1776; a downtrodden people pushing greatly for the right to life, liberty and the pursuit of happiness. Americans would do well to study the society there, perhaps they will find something they might have forgot.

Perhaps it is something of value—that place. More than sand and death. Perhaps it is a light in a corner of the world known for its oppressive and omnipotent dark. Perhaps it is a light worth preserving.

13 September 2018: Rimêlan, Rojava:

I cooked yesterday, & in the afternoon we heard that we were going to play a soccer match in Rimêlan. Giddy, excited simply by leaving The Academy, we piled into the car in our uniforms, holding our rifles. & we showed up to the fields & these fucks we were to play were all wearing matching jerseys. They looked like the damned official YPG soccer team. "We're supposed to play them? They're wearing cleats!" During the first half, I was goalkeeper. I held them off from scoring for as long as I could, but it was a barrage of shots. & just as I started to get cocky, the first hit the net. Then another. Then another. Then another. All abruptly just before halftime. We couldn't keep the ball on their side of the field for more than a touch or 2, & they hit home on 3 shots. In the second half I moved to wing. The ball began to be played much more forward & before long, a combination of myself, Soro, & Dilsoz proved too much & we finally scored a goal. But then they scored 2 more: YPG International 1-6 YPG Rimêlan. Hîwa was running down the sidelines—well, clunking down them in his oversized hiking boots, tripped & fell face-first onto the rocky pitch. He stood up, pretending to be fine, with blood pouring from a nasty cut on his chin. Then there was a high-arching air ball. I went for it, & so did an opponent. He hit me in the face with the back of his head & I immediately knew I was hurt. Blood spurting all over my HD Salvage shirt. My bottom teeth went through my lip. In the hospital they gave me 4 stitches, Hîwa 6.

"You're a hero Azad; you were wounded in the war!" - Dilsoz, inspecting my stitches.

* * *

Of course, only I would do it playing what was supposed to be a fun game of soccer. Now I cannot eat or talk, & my mouth hangs open like a yokel's. Hîwa & I went to Dêrik with Canşêr, got cleaned up & given some drugs. We didn't spend much time around town, left, had some çay with logistics hevals–they didn't have the Rojava flag we were looking for. Kawa came for supper. It was good to see him again. He should be headed to Hajin within the week. Lucky bastard; as for us, we keep waiting.

Warren Stoddard II

In a Crater Holding the Pin of a Grenade

It was all ringing. It was all dust. It was all so many things and the ground seemed to tilt and I felt myself stumble over a fallen brick and slam against the wall. I could feel the heat sizzling off shrapnel. From outside I felt the ground reverberate again, then again. Like the steady crank of an oil derrick.

On my hands and knees now, I fumbled around in the rubble for my rifle. Sunlight streamed in through the bifurcated wall, spilling into the cloud of dust. Milk in water, I thought. A child's doll had fallen from a wooden dresser, the dresser itself scarred by metal fragments. Clothes were strewn about, collecting dust. Beige. Ashen. Eggshell. I coughed, rising from my hands and knees with my rifle in hand again before slouching down and carefully picking my way through the strewn bricks and fabric, feeling the ground roll beneath me. I called out.

Ringing.

The earth trembled again.

In the corner of the room, now growing brighter in the dissipating dust, I found him. He was slouched in the door-frame, holding his rifle between his knees. His eyes were wide. I touched his shoulder, and he turned to me, startled. He jumped backward.

He must have said something to me.

But I shook my head. I pointed to my ears.

He smiled. He pointed to himself.

Ringing.

In the next room I saw the flicker of the lights of the handheld radio. Our last man was shouting into it silently. The tendons in his neck were bulging. Veins in his forehead throbbed. He slammed his fist against the cinderblock wall behind him. So we had all made it.

He rose and walked toward me. He set his hand on my shoulder and I could feel it trembling. He looked me up and down, shook his head, nodded, looked me over again.

I thought I saw his lips mouth the words, "Are you alright?"

And I nodded in return. Then I pointed to my ears and shook my head.

He grinned. He leaned very close to me and I could feel the air vibrate against my throat as he shouted. He leaned away again, gave me a look as if to ask if I had heard.

I shook my head.

I saw his lips move again. "Fucking Americans," he had said.

We both laughed.

The earth still trembled. He picked up his rifle and we grabbed the third of our team. The man with the radio was named Tolhildan. This I remembered. I was not sure that I could recall my own nom de guerre, and I had only met this third of us this morning, but I knew the man with the radio was Tolhildan, so I followed him.

We wound our way toward the wall where the missile had hit. Tolhildan gestured to it, looked back at us, and flung his hand in contempt. He pointed to the ceiling and made a motion with his palm to suggest it may collapse. Then he waved for us to follow and we stepped out through the destroyed wall and into the crater that the missile had made. It was deep. Deep enough that you could have set a now-silent elephant in the bottom. Beyond it, dusty plains stretched to the west where our enemy was holed up in the city of Manbij. You could see black pennants fluttering in the wind. To our left and right were more hovels like the destroyed one we had been stationed in. They made up a solidly defined frontline. How had the American jets missed their target so badly?

We could still feel the earth trembling steadily, and Tolhildan now sat at the base of the crater, swinging a purple backpack around to his lap and fishing around in it for something. When the other man and I had joined him at the bottom, Tolhildan presented two cans of spicy tuna, a pack of bread, and a green bell pepper. He set them in the center of us and winked, smiling.

I could still feel the earth trembling. Concussion after concussion. Mortarbursts.

It was a strange thing, but without the sound of incoming rounds, the battlefield took on a certain kind of placidity. There was no sound of tearing paper. You could not tell when shells were coming or when they were going. You could not tell if they would land close or if they would land far. You only felt the ground swell. The sand shook. Somewhere, they were hitting, but you would not know if it would be you, and if it were to be you, you would have no time to get out of the way. There was no more fear. Fear would have done nothing for us now. Fear could not save us. So I ate.

We tore the pieces of nan, using them to scoop up the tuna. We passed around the bell pepper, each taking a bite before handing it to the next man. We sat close together as though it were a bitterly cold night and these cans of tuna were all the fire we had to keep us warm until dawn.

I was reminded of so many picnics in my youth where the meal had been delayed so that some mother or father could run to the store and pick up a pack of plastic silverware. They would return to distribute it all from little cardboard boxes, the knives and spoons and forks rattling tinnily. You would eat potato salad and coleslaw. You would eat cake. Maybe you would eat ice cream too—a-la-mode. Here we ate with our hands. I licked the hot sauce of the tuna from my fingers and reached for more bread.

Above, the sky was a circle of blue through the mouth of the crater. I could see the crisscrossing spaghetti-noodle vapor trails from the jets and prayed that one would not come back for us.

There was still so much ringing.

Leaning back from the food, I lit a cigarette and checked the action of my rifle. From across the crater, Tolhildan jabbed his chin at me questioningly.

"My ears are broken," I said in Kurdish. But I could not hear the sounds I made. It felt as though I were humming. My voice was locked in my chest. I gestured at my ears.

Tolhildan lifted his chin toward the other man, who still sat wide-eyed and faraway. He did not answer, so Tolhildan looked back to me as if to ask, "Him too?"

"Erê," I said: Yes. Nodding, feeling it hum in my chest. I took a drag from the cigarette and flicked it away. I looked up toward the sky again.

The first yellows of sunset were beginning to creep into that circular field of blue. I wondered if the birds would be singing even amid the battle. I wondered if I might have felt their songs vibrate against my shoulder had the mortars not thudded so consistently. Birdsong had never begun a war, I thought. But there in the crater the war had ended for me, at least for the day, and I wondered how it would be to return home from the war, bringing nothing from it but a flag and old dirty patches and the ringing in my ears. What could I do? Go home and do what? I could stand at the floor of an aviary, deaf, the songs of the birds stifled and my perception of them somehow stunted, but the grace of a bent wing on an updraft would hold as much grace as any sheet of written music, each wheeling and alighting a fermata or crescendo, and every hawk or warbler or sparrow or mockingbird a treble clef or simple note, and their paths through the sky a series of well-aligned glissandos.

Then suddenly as night fell I became very afraid that I may never hear the sound of music again, and that any grace I might find in my life would come only from the circling motion of a bird on the wind.

The stars burned through. The percussion of the mortarbursts faltered and then halted altogether. The earth was still. The air was gentle. And not hearing it overhead, the first wave of tracer rounds looked like fireflies in midsummer. Red or green. Bright orange. Their flights over the mouth of the crater would leave any man mesmerized. They were sirens, only this time as you were lashed to the mast you could hear nothing; their song was a vision. It was simple clarity, cutting back and forth across the night sky above us. I longed to take my rifle and flip down the safety and join in that optical symphony, and in all the years that may be to come in my life I knew I would regret not having done so, pleading with circumstance that one more round could have been fired in anger, *one more*. But without my ears in that place and time I would have been nothing but an angry and unrestrained nuisance in any firefight.

In the darkness I could have been anywhere. Had the tracers halted and hung frozen in the sky above us we might have been seated in the sand in Malta at Christmastime. We might have been in Novgorod could I not feel the film of dirt on my neck. We might have been in Munich had we only been able to hear and never recall the horrors of yesterday. It was only then that I remembered we were lame ducks, seated in a crater, our only hope that the enemy could not advance on our positions, that we could make it to the calm air of morning without Daesh fighters pouring into our hole and binding our hands and decapitating us on video for our loved ones to see. It was only then that the fear returned. I felt around my belt for a grenade. Finding it, I held it in my hand, feeling the tightness of the pin, envisioning pulling it, dropping the spoon as we were overrun, feeling the air swell and then the emptiness that came after that. It would be better to be a thousand free shards than a single imprisoned vase. I held it tightly.

We tried to sleep in shifts, but Tolhildan would hardly let himself blink. He knew that we could hear nothing and I think it made him very afraid. Worse than any shrapnel-whistling close call.

Eventually the tracers died out. The sky became still again. The world turned quietly. Faint reverberations from far-off airstrikes patted at our backs from the ground beneath, and I let myself drift to sleep, still clutching the grenade, wishing that I could see or hear anything beyond that maw of night above me. Thinking of home as a silent film, remembering the sound of voices.

I woke with a start, squeezing my finger on the pin. Tolhildan was still awake, and in the dim light of early morning he lifted his palms toward me and nodded reassurance. I was breathing heavily. I relaxed my grip on the pin. I breathed deeply and felt the calmness of morning, the cool air, the muted clouds of dust.

An hour later the morning light was fully in the gray air and the three of us all knew that we would have to leave the crater soon. I knew that it would be my last day in the war and wished very badly that it might never end, that there might be some great final barrage we would run through, that we would have to fight our way out of that circle of 10,000 jihadis waving black flags, that I might somehow become stuck there as the gears in a fine wristwatch follow the same perpetual loop. I did not want the war to end and at the same time I longed so profoundly to go home. I did not understand it in that moment, and I am sure that in all the moments to come I will come no closer to understanding than a cartoon coyote comes to a roadrunner.

I wondered if there was any cowardice in leaving. But I could not hear myself speak. I became horribly frightened again at thinking of how I would learn to live this way. War had been easy in comparison. What in the hell was I supposed to do? But I suppose you only ever place the next foot forward.

I hoped now that they would overrun our position. I hoped I would have to pull the pin, that my comrades and I would share a last look of understanding and all willingly walk into that sacrifice. Tolhildan would. I was sure of that.

Then I saw his ears perk up, and he turned to me. He lifted a single finger to his lips, gesturing to keep quiet. He pointed over the rim of the crater, opened and closed his palm. Voices. My grip tightened on the grenade. Tolhildan saw this, looked me in the eye, and nodded.

There it was.

And as we sat I saw the profiles of two heads crest the rim of the crater, coming from the building we had occupied. Seeing me, one ducked back, pulling his friend with him. I pulled the pin of the grenade, waiting to drop the spoon until I could be sure. They peeked again at us over the edge of the crater. This time their rifles were raised. They had no patches on their uniforms—they were filthy.

I was waiting for some final sign. Tolhildan was speaking to them rapidly, gesturing furiously. His rifle lay in his lap. Looking down my knuckles were white, and then the sun broke over the crater rim, drenching the world in fluorescence. I felt my ears ringing still, and I wished only that I could instead hear the birdsong I knew would be in the trees while feeling the spoon of the grenade dig into the palm of my hand, then fade as my grip loosened.

2 October 2018: The Academy, Rojava:

"Fuck the president! I ask the sexiest questions in America! Hannah why'd you leave me?!" - One of Alîşer's marching cadences.

At the end of PT this morning, as we were marching back towards the Academy, we were targeted. Someone had left a litter of puppies there at the front of the driveway in the short span of time we were away, knowing full well we would take care of them. Bastards. They are cute though. We carried them home & passed them around as we stretched. Then I mixed them some milk & Aşîtî & I fed them. Some are smart enough to drink from a saucer, but the consensus is that many of the puppies will not make it. "Dogs in Syria don't last."

29 December 2018: Qereçox, Rojava:

That dog leapt & writhed in the air as if it'd been shot. We'd tracked it from the other side of the nokta, from the boulder-filled ravine to where it lay in the valley basking in the sun on the banks of the river at the opposite end of the field. Bahoz had to be sure it didn't belong to some shepherd, & I was sure it did not. He took the first shot from some 125 meters away. I thought he'd gotten it by the way the animal reacted, its pepper-gray body jerking to & fro in the air. But then it hit the ground & bolted. First it bounded across the river & then began a headlong sprint up the mountainside. I fired. The wild dog let out a scream like none I have ever heard. I saw no telltale puff of dirt that would've betrayed that either of us had missed, but the dog did not stop running, only a slight change in its momentum. Bahoz fired again & I laughed at the ridiculousness of the situation as I let fly another round.

"If you take violent men & keep them penned up somewhere where they have nothing to do & no way to relieve that pressure, before long the whole thing will begin to burst at the seams until they start doing dumb shit." – Soro around the hookah tonight.

At least that dog won't be coming back. I wish I'd just opened up on the pack the night I had the chance. At least then we'd know for sure one was dead. This one may be as well, somewhere over the crest of the mountain, but that doesn't put any meat on the table.

29 November 2018: Qereçox, Rojava, Noktaya Şehîd Kendal Breizh:

It was shortly after I adjusted my rifle sling on nobet that the puppies began shrieking. Soon a roaring cacophony of grown dogs joined in. I ran across the compound to find 4 dogs jabbing in & out like a pit of snakes over one dog pinned to the ground. The half-moon was obscured by clouds. All there was to see were shapes & shades of fur. I threw a small brick into the whirling mass... nothing happened. Still the snarling & shrieking. A bigger brick too was useless. I unslung & took my rifle off safe. The mamma dog was somewhere in that pile, & I couldn't shoot Leyla, so I fired one off into the air & went full hick, waving my arms about like a rabid castaway flagging down a ship, "Go on! Git! Get yer ass on outta here!" You could hear the shot echoing off the walls of the valley below, inundating the night with disquiet. & the dogs scattered. The adrenaline was pumping pretty good. The momma wasn't hurt too bad in the morning. Just some scratches. & the puppies are safe.

Warren Stoddard II

A Line on a Map

The cages of the chickens in the bed of the truck made a poor pillow for his head, but his eyes kept growing heavy and falling closed. *Gelhat,* he told himself. Whatever he had been called before was of little importance. *My name is Gelhat now*.

Through the darkness, he could see the others in the back of the truck. All told, they were thirteen, crushed together like sardines, sweating, shoulders rubbing together in the cramped space. The air was stuffy and hot, feathers fluttered fitfully in the wind, sticking to sweaty arms. Each time the truck hit a bump in the road, its passengers were flung into one another, startled chickens clucked around them. A man across the aisle tapped Gelhat on the arm and pointed to his own wrist.

"I think he wants you to take your watch off," the Italian next to Gelhat said.

Gelhat looked down at the ring of luminescence on his wrist and back at the Italian. It was 10 PM. I forget what his name is, he thought as he unfastened the watch and tucked it into the pocket of his jeans. "Are we still in Iraq?" Gelhat asked.

"I think so," the Italian answered. "Do you remember my new name?"

"I was just wondering the same thing."

"It's Botan," the Canadian said from across the aisle. His head was in his hands, his palms working to burrow into his eyes. His knees were pressed tightly together, and his beret had fallen from his head into the aisle of feet in the bed of the truck. "How do you not remember your name?"

Gelhat stayed quiet.

"Well I only just got it," Botan said over the rattle of the truck. He turned to Gelhat and whispered, "I cannot stand this fucking guy."

The trio had left a safe house in a city in Iraq earlier that day. They were handed from one stranger to another when a taxi came to pick them up. The driver spoke no English, but the first stranger assured them that they were going to be taken into Syria by this man. They had no choice but to trust him. They loaded in the car and it took them from the fast-moving city to gently rolling golden Iraqi fields of late June. They stopped for energy drinks and snacks along the way, and twice for the Canadian to shit. His stomach had not adjusted to the new food yet. In the months to come, they would all have their fair share of shitting episodes—this was only the first.

The Canadian sat white-faced and silent the whole ride, grinding his teeth and tapping his feet on the floorboard. The American and the Italian talked sparsely, and they tried to chat with the driver, but he spoke a different dialect of Kurmanji than they had studied before coming here. So he played them music. They napped, and they stared out the window when they were awake. The land went from rolling fields of hay to flat arid desert and back to rolling hills again. The whole surface was baked by the sun.

They stopped at checkpoints staffed by AK-wielding soldiers, handed over their passports, and watched the guards with as much an air of innocent tourism as the westerners could muster while each soldier inspected their documents and craned their necks into the driver's window to stare in amazement at the white men in the car. Tourists in Iraq? "Whoa! America good!" They would give a thumbs up and send the car on its way.

And then quite suddenly, they were in the mountains. The flat expanse of rolling highway turned to one narrow and winding road. From that to another bumpier one that cut hard switchbacks between the trees lining the path. Finally, they stopped. The driver held his hands up as a signal for the trio to wait in the car. He dismounted and jogged somewhere within the forest.

The Italian and American looked at each other. The beret-headed Canadian grinded his thighs together and peeked over the edge of the windowsill. "Here he comes," he said.

"*Heval,*" the driver said through a thick Kurdish accent as he jumped back into the car, "drones." He gestured with his hands toward the sky. "Turkey. *Ne baş.*" Not good.

The American nodded his head. The driver captured his gaze and gestured behind him to where several olive-dressed figures stood in the shadow of the trees. The driver pointed to them and said, "Friends."

The Italian, Canadian and American all shook their heads in understanding. "*Erê. Baş*. Yes. Good," they said.

The driver pressed a button beneath the steering wheel to open the back hatch of the car where their bags were stowed, and he waved them away. "*Serkeftin*," he said. "Go! Go!"

They quickly opened the doors of the car and shouldered their backpacks. The Canadian carried two smaller bags, the American a light travel ruck, and the Italian an overstuffed duffel bag with straps stitched to it. They jogged to the tree line and were greeted by three green-dressed men and a woman with an AK slung over her shoulder. These Kurds wore loose, baggy pants, olive shirts, and GI-style jackets. A sash of lighter green was tied about each of their waists. They eyed the westerners suspiciously. Colorful scarves were draped over their heads and shoulders.

"*Merheba, heval*," said one of them. "Come. Follow us. Stay under tree. Drones in sky. *Turkîyê*." He gestured above him. The westerners nodded and followed the Kurds like baby ducklings, each of them periodically peering up at the sky through the leaves of the trees as they walked.

"Stop!" said the woman. The westerners froze. She held up both of her palms towards them and then tapped at one of her ears as she raised it skyward.

The westerners, in palm-sweating silence, did the same. As they tilted their heads to the sky, they heard it—the low churning murmur of the drone, very quietly circling the air above them like mechanized doom. The air was stagnant, the forest silent but for the droning, ever-growing pulse of the aircraft above them. The westerners stood breathless, softly pushing the air from their lungs in shallow exhales, afraid that if they breathed too heavily the beast in the sky may detect a change in the winds, turn round and unleash a fiery cataclysm upon their group huddled in the forest. But its sound grew dimmer now. It faded toward the northern horizon. And then came a soft thud—as though someone had dropped a textbook in a classroom down the hall from that forest. Then silence. The green-clad Kurds looked at one another with sadness, then to the westerners. "Come," one of them said.

The seven made their way winding through oaks and tall pines down a slope, and they came to a clearing and stopped. They could see another of the green-dressed guerillas on the other side of the glade. He waved and looked to the sky with his arms outspread and shrugged to the group. He ushered them through the clearing. As they came to the other side, he shook each of their hands, "*Xêr hatî*," he said.

"Welcome," translated the man who spoke English. The group followed this new stranger through the underbrush that soon became thick with shrubs and Mediterranean undergrowth. A path had been walked here many times. It was a thin snake of white dirt between the green. In the distance, the westerners could hear water running, people chatting quietly. They came to a marsh and were led over a rickety bridge constructed of repurposed shipping pallets. Turtles swam below them in a brook of clear-running water.

On the other side of the bridge a line of people awaited them. The westerners and their Kurdish guides shook each of their hands and exchanged welcomes. The three westerners were made to sit at plastic tables under a thatch wood awning. The air was cool from the stream, and precise light from the now setting sun cut through the trees to their west, setting hard shadows on the ground beneath their feet.

The Kurds offered their guests hot, sweetened tea, followed by a course of pasta. Through the translator, they told jokes and asked the westerners their names. They could pronounce none of them. To make the sounds with their tongues proved near impossible.

"No. It will not work," the translator said to the American. He laughed, "We cannot make this noise."

The Kurdish woman next to the American said something to the interpreter.

"She says she wants to free you from this name." The translator laughed again and spoke to the woman in Kurdish.

She touched the American on the arm. "Your name," she said, "*Gelhat*."

The American, now Gelhat looked up bewildered at the translator. "What does it mean?" he asked.

The translator whispered to the woman. She turned to Gelhat.

"*The people come*."

"You are now Heval Gelhat. It is a very good name, heval."

The Canadian was given the name of Rodî, the Italian–Botan. They ate sweet desserts glazed with honey. They sang songs. They learned Kurdish dances beneath the shade of that thatched shelter as the sun fell. The guerillas were smiling, the drone strikes all but forgotten, as though the only way to stave off certain death were to dance.

Gelhat woke as the truck began to slow. The men and women sardined with him in the bed of the truck pressed fingers to their lips gesturing silence. The women tightened their grips on their rifles. The brakes squeaked as the truck slowed to a halt. The rattling of the vehicle went still–Gelhat could hear a muffled conversation in Kurdish above the soft cooing of the chickens, he could smell his own fear above their stench. Those around him held their breath. In the dark they moved their eyes slowly from end to end of the rows of passengers lined on the benches of the truck. They did not blink.

The muffled conversation outside the truck quieted. Footsteps could be heard receding into the distance. Through a gap in the mass of feathers, Gelhat could see light illuminating asphalt beside the truck. They were stopped at a checkpoint. The engine was turned off. The night was silent. What would the guard do when he came back? Gelhat worried, frozen rigid by fear and acceptance as one who has never flown jams themselves tight into the seat of the plane. Would the guard check the bed of the truck, thrust chicken cages aside? Had the guerillas handed him a bribe? What if the guard wasn't happy with the amount, ripped open the canvas roof of the truck and shined a bright flashlight in the faces of those being smuggled to Rojava?

Gelhat would bolt for it, he decided. He would force his way through the crush of people, past the Kalashnikov-wielding women and the guard, out into the night, and he would run. He would hide in the brush, panting, an American alone in Iraq, thousands of his countrymen had died here, what would another matter? They would uncover him from his hideout—they would either shoot him, and he would never see the end coming, or they would cuff him, throw him in jail with all the other dregs drained from the dust of Mesopotamia.

What had he been thinking? To come here, to the Middle East, to fight for a cause and a country he had never seen, to *die* for it? You have trusted your life to these strangers, he thought. You are in the bed of the truck with 15 people who have never seen Texas, two of which speak English, and they are supposed to take you to *Syria*. Fucking Syria. Yes, *that* Syria. You could get blown up at any minute by Turkish drones or any million of the other ways to die in the Levant. You are completely out of all control. You are gone from the safety and comfort of the life you once led. Your life is at the whims of this fucked up world now. You are hiding in a goddamned chicken truck with a dozen people you have never met, and you can barely remember your new alias.

Footsteps approached. Shallow breaths. And the engine started. The people huddled in the bed of the truck let out a collective sigh of relief as the wheels beneath them began to turn and the frame of the vehicle started to rattle and the high shrieking of highway wind again muffled any sound they might make.

Before long, Botan began to doze, and Gelhat let the Italian's head rest on his shoulder. He leaned his own head back against the uncomfortable wire cages for the duration of the ride. After a while he again felt the wheels transition from high-speed highway to winding, narrow road, and finally to a trundling pace across loose gravel.

They were made to dismount from the feathered bed of the truck, they grabbed their bags from the bed of another and shouldered them again. In the distance they could hear the mechanical workings of a factory. Its lights were a soft white glow on the horizon. Brighter lights lined the rise of a hill to their south. A fence could be seen running beneath them. A full moon shone above. Jesus, this whole place is lit up like Christmas, Gelhat thought. He and the others headed to Rojava followed a man single file into the cool darkness of the small valley of a river. In the reeds beside the water, there were men standing in the shadows—black figures holding AK-47s. They looked on as the file meandered past them. The westerners and the Kurds stepped as carefully as they could across the round river stones beneath their feet, but their march across the banks sounded like the dropping of rocks on glass. Any slip of step would ring out like a landslide.

The man at the front of the procession held up his hands, signaling the group to stop. Some sat down among the pebbles, others squatted, and those hidden in the reeds stood, scanning the river. On the other side, an incline rose sharply from a narrow and densely forested bank. At the top of the hill, Gelhat could see a square stone structure. The silhouette of a triangular flag fluttered above it.

There it is, he thought. Just across the border. Just across this river. This river that before now only existed in geography textbooks and history lessons. This, one of the two rivers that birthed civilization. You are about to cross it. And your life is like a movie now, isn't it? Normal people do not do this shit. To anyone at home you are *crazy*. He took some comfort in that. But the night was peaceful—quiet. He took a deep breath. He sat back as quietly as he could, leaning against the pad of his pack, and he smiled through nervousness and satisfaction. He picked up a stone and turned it over in his hands. The stars were dim. The full moon washed the whole scene in a white dye. Gelhat carefully turned to look back at the dark men in the shadows holding their rifles. Four that he could see. He wondered how all this would work. Maybe they would row. Maybe they would be ferried across under that bright moon. How was this secretive? Certainly, they could have picked a better time for this, a better place. That moon, those lights so bright. He eased himself a little further into the shadow of the reeds, still turning the rock in his hands.

Would they be lined up and shot? It would be so easy for them, Gelhat thought. Just mow us down, here and now. It was only three emails. You exchanged three emails with this group, and you now trust anything they would say to you. What do they care for you? How could they trust you, how could you trust them? But what would they have to lie about? They do have quite a great many enemies in the world. A Kurd needs every friend he can get.

He dropped the rock.

And he could feel the eyes turn and pierce into him, trying to will the noise away, to shove it down and subdue it. Gelhat heard footsteps receding over the rocks in the shadows behind him. There was a far-off baying of a dog. And then the roar of a motor–close and condemning. There was a rustle among them all. The westerners eyed each other–the whites of their eyes bright in the moonlight–contemplating running. They faced the river. A quiet burbling of anticipation rose in those Kurds around them. The men with the rifles moved to different positions.

In the front of the line of people, three were made to stand. They were shuffled through the shadows to the shore of the Tigris by the silhouette of a man. A boat emerged from around the bend with its wake rippling the glass surface of that river, the moon's rays now distorted in its reflection. It nosed into the bank and its driver ushered the three over the edge of the little rubber dinghy and across the water. Once it reached the other bank, the motor went silent, the boat nosed in behind the silhouette of a tree, and then it started again, growing louder as it made its way back to the Iraqi side of the river. The wake of the boat again sent ripples over the glass surface of the Tigris.

Another group of three loaded in, and they were ferried across. The boat returned. The hollow hum of the factory flowed over the horizon.

Gelhat stood at the upward wave of a hand. Beside him, Botan and Rodî shouldered their backpacks. The volunteers followed the dark figure of a man down to the bank of the river. From the dinghy, he pulled out three life jackets. He buckled one on himself and handed one out to each of the others. He took their packs and tossed them next to the captain of the dinghy. Gelhat pulled his life vest over his head.

Its nylon fabric was rough, bleached and irradiated by years of sun. It smelled of an antique store. The buckles were broken. Botan and Rodî stepped over the edge and into the boat. Gelhat took hold of a hand and it pulled him in.

The floor of the vessel was taut. Its sides were filled with enough air to burst, but they kept it above water. The captain pushed the boat away from the shallows with an oar, then started the motor. The black rubber dinghy glided elegantly across the surface of the water. Gelhat sat at the prow of the boat, looking out across the river. He knew behind him the Iraqi bank would be receding in the distance–the wake of the boat morphing the glass waters of the slow-moving Tigris. Before him, the Syrian bank of the river rose like approaching mountains in the night. The motor of the boat cut, and in silence the dinghy, propelled by its momentum, nosed softly behind a tree and onto the bank. In the boat, the westerners were made to remove their life jackets. As Gelhat turned to shore he saw the figure of a man standing in the shadows. Gelhat took hold of another outstretched hand, and it pulled him to land. The man's face broke into a smile and he spoke in English.

"Welcome to Rojava."

25 October 2018: The Academy, Rojava:

I drew a good lot on my day as cook. It got me out of a hard day of PT, & I only had to listen to people read their reports for an hour & a half. The new Şahîn helped me at lunch & supper—nice fella from Sicily. We jammed out to music while we cut vegetables. Lots of Fleetwood Mac. & for supper I cooked the St. Crispin's Day feast: a whole 9 kilos of lamb, mixed with some potatoes—Kendal's recipe, & a separate plate for the vegetarians. It's the first red meat I've had since the Eid.

"& gentlemen in England now a-bed
Shall think themselves accurs'd they were not here,
& hold their manhoods cheap whiles any speaks
That fought with us upon Saint Crispin's day."
-William Shakespeare: Henry V.

Hîwa & I acted out a scene from Henry V before I gave the old " Şiyarben xweş û jîyanbê." It was the loudest I've ever heard them respond, "Saxbê!" Chills ran down my spine. It felt cool, dammit. It felt good. As though we are finally off at the front. The dream of it is still there that we will play a part in this war—something tangible & important. Every day closer to the military training we get, the higher our morale is. Soon. So soon we will be out of this fucking Academy & in the tabûr. Then a fever pitch of greetings & goodbyes before—inshallah—we will be on operations. We will be fighting in Hajin. We will not rest until we are at the front. Those of us that want the fight are so ravenous for it that I think there is no way we cannot attain it. We will fight. We must fight. It is what we came here to do. & then in some far-off future I will be on my way home to fight an entirely different kind of war that operates on an entirely different set of rules. & I think it will be much harder to make it there. I am looking forward to the future for the first time in a long time—maybe since that flight here. We are all going through this together—mutual suffering. Nothing brings people closer than that. How can I leave my friends? Any man in ages hence must curse himself he was not here, yet even if he does, he will not understand what it is he is lacking. He will never understand this feeling, why it was & is worth sacrificing so much, no matter how hard he might try. War is so much more than suffering. It is the bonds which war forges that are heralded in the songs poets write. Down below the surface is all that could ever matter, but things must end one day. & I will leave. I will go home & live a happy life carrying these things with me. I hope I am strong enough to do that.

Warren Stoddard II

Or the Lack of It

I remember her standing there in the kitchen. Her brown hair was around her shoulders, glasses over green eyes. Her shorts were short, and her shirt was loose fitting–it was mine.

"Are you sure you don't want any help?" I asked.

The cutting board was littered with vegetables: peppers, onions, hatch green chilies. Next to it was a bowl of mixed cheeses and a saucer full of Old El Paso enchilada sauce.

"No," she said. "I'm pretty much finished. You always wait until the work is done to ask."

"Well usually you don't want any help."

"I get along just fine without help. You'd probably only mess it all up anyway," she said.

I put my hands around her slim waist and pressed my lips to the crook of her neck. "We couldn't have that," I said. "Besides, you make the best enchiladas." I kissed her higher on the neck.

"Stop it," she teased and slapped playfully at me with the flat side of a knife. "You're distracting me."

I let go of her waist and walked around the kitchen island to the living room and plopped down on the couch. I laced my fingers together behind my head and sighed towards the ceiling with my feet kicked up on the arm rest of the sofa.

"After all, this is my last meal in the states." She was quiet. I studied the pattern in the cloth of the pastel pink cushions of the sofa and then looked around the walls at the hanging decorations of pastel and subdued hues. She always had an eye for decorating. I again looked at her—her face was drawn and tense. "What's the matter?" I asked, knowing the answer.

"Nothing," she said as she stuffed the tortillas with the cheese mixture and rolled them into cylinders in a pan.

I knew she was lying, but we all lie and tell ourselves things believing that it is possible to confuse the mind into submission and trick it into believing what we wish reality to be.

The ceiling fan was whirring and the bearings within had lost enough grease that every so often I could hear a creak. The air in the room was cool. The light from within the oven emanating from the kitchen added a rich atmosphere of anticipation to the air. I knew dinner would be ready soon when I heard the oven door open and then close. I could feel the heat smoothly spill into the space. I heard her sniffling.

Still staring at the ceiling, I told her not to be sad.

"How could I not be sad?"

"Well you're going to be sad about the damned thing either way. And it doesn't make sense to be sad when I *am* still here and there are still some good times to be had." I looked at her. The sniffling had stopped and was replaced by somber nodding. Her eyes were bloodshot and stared back into my own. "Come here," I said, and slapped my hand on the backrest of the sofa as playfully as I could.

The next day I was going to war. There would be little contact with her while I was gone—perhaps none. I would have to face life and death, eternity or the lack of it—without her. Without her. The sadness, the glory, the waiting, the banners in the wind; things men who have never been to war often imagine it is filled with. But the honesty of war would challenge the whole notion or the idea of the thing. That is why it makes such great men of boys. It forces you to accept your situation at a glance. It is brutally honest and simple—you have no choice but to accept it; and often when this acceptance is reached in the honesty of the surroundings, boys who become men often come to a stop, simultaneously, instantaneously, spending their final moment indulging in the very human urge to wish that things were different. There is no use in wishing, your lot is cast and you are stuck with it. You did not go left, but right. It will never be any other way. Tell death as you saw it, as you see it. In your honesty there is something important in the human condition that has always been weathering away. Eternity, or the lack of it, is nothing to be feared. It is a fate and a realization that every man before you and every man after you must realize. Death is but the end of something, yet it is only as final as you believe it to be. In the end it will be what it is. There is no way of knowing until you get there and there is no use in spending your life, your whole life, your *only* life fretting over the end of you or of anyone else. Enjoy it and make the most of it while you have it and sort everything else out later. For god's sake do *something*. Make it true. And maybe you will find some meaning in the honesty.

She was sitting in my lap with her arms draped around me like I was wearing her as a necklace. Her golden-green eyes were staring into mine; and the worry in them was gone now—replaced by something else.

"How long until the enchiladas are done?"

She looked over the backrest of the couch, "About seventeen minutes to kill. What should we do?"

I lifted her and carried her with her arms still clasped around my neck from the couch to the bedroom with my lips welded to hers. And our clothes became a pile on the floor. And I could feel the heat of her skin on mine—the slopes of her hip bones—the tenderness of her breasts pressed against my own chest—me pressing her down—and her pulling me deeper into the well of that passion like a siren to a passing ship in the Aegean or the Tyrol or the Mediterranean or the Sea of Cortez or the Red. Red, red rocks approaching the bow—looming timidly, honestly, viscously. Impossible to escape, but so necessary to put off and keep above water for as long as you can until they rip through your hull like so many bullets I have now seen, shaking the whole ship violently and with all the power of a god behind them until the bulkheads take on water and your vessel begins to submerge deep to the ocean floor with a quiet, empty, and if you are lucky, warm whimper.

We lay there in that familiar breathless silence after lovemaking until we heard the timer of the oven ding from the kitchen.

She pulled on another of my shirts and rose from that bed and pulled the tray of enchiladas from the oven and set them on the counter to cool. I went to join her there. I poured two glasses of water. I set out the forks and the plates and a small tub of sour cream, and she started to cry again.

I held her.

And once the food was on the plates and smothered in cool sour cream her tears stopped. And we ate and it was good and each bite was relished and given a satisfied "mmm." I had not long been lying in bed awake that night before she turned over to me and held me tight to her in a manner that seemed to declare that she would never let me go if possible, but she knew that I would have to leave. And we stayed that way—quiet, peaceful, and awake until sometime into the night.

And now in the airport there is a crowd thrumming around us in hurried movement. So we cannot be as two lovers are when they are alone. We are filling these last bittersweet moments with idle chatter and it is killing me more painfully than any bullet I may ever take.

The crowd begins to thicken and grow as a pot may boil—starting slowly, then it seems to suddenly happen all at once just as you look away. I am staring into her eyes that are quickly becoming bloodshot and filling with tears at the thought of me taking that fatal step away towards the security queue. I wish that I could put into words how I feel about her here, but it only comes out in that oft repeated and watered down eight-letter phrase. I hold her close to me with finality before I step away. And just before I reach the man who asks to see my boarding pass, I turn around and grab her and sweep her from her feet and plant one last, good kiss on her lips. I can feel her tears on my cheeks and know that they are mixing with my own. I say goodbye through a thick voice and a stuffy nose and look away.

I walk forward with hot eyes as the man checks my ticket and waves me through. I look forward as I walk back and forth in the serpentine arrangement of blue extendo-bands that you see only in movie theaters and airports.

And then something happens in front of me. The line stops and I am pulled with resistance by some force to look around and behind me. A woman in a wheelchair has set off the metal detectors. There is some kind of row about this.

Slowly, I turn my gaze back to her. And her eyes meet mine. There is something burning in them that cannot be defined. Then I wave to her, meekly. And her eyes soften, and she waves back to me with more pity in her eyes than a child leaving grandmother's house who cannot stop staring through the back window of the car even long after the house and grandmother are gone from view. There we stand like that, even as the line starts to slowly shuffle forward again. For what seems an eternity we stare at one another across that distance.

And then I look forward and hand my boarding pass to another security guard, trying to harden my eyes. And then I remove my shoes, my belt, all keys and foreign objects from my pockets. I step through the metal detector and out the other side with a pathetic wave, looking in her direction. I think I see her golden-green eyes through the crowd of people. Her hand shoots desperately above the crowd like it might grasp mine one final time.

I remember she was wearing blue–my shirt.

5 November 2018: Çîyayê Qereçox, Rojava:

The art of recon is complex, requiring many skills & subtle nuances. In the Marine Corps, to learn this art you must spend nearly a year in training. We got it covered in about 5 hours. Ideological lessons were quick & done by 9:30. I finished <u>*Shantaram*</u> *during the lunch break. In the afternoon the hills were being pelted by bullet sized drops of rain. I wore no heavy winter coat; embrace the suck. In the training exercise, we sneaked to the village. The team I took charge of went halfway up the slopes of the mountain & found a position by an oil pump. The mud was slathered on thick to our ankles. But the position was no good—an obstructed view. So we moved out, but quickly came on 40 meters of open ground. Time to crawl. The cold of the mud seeped through my pants & quickly caked my weapon in a coat of brown ooze. I looked back & flashed the group a big smile. Demhat & Breizh had painted their faces with earth. We continued to crawl until we were under protection of a ridgeline. I took up an observation post while the rest—Aşîtî Breizh, & Bahoz—kept security. We watched the village for an hour, keeping track of the comings & goings of the townsfolk. When it came time to move out back to the meeting point, mists hugged the slopes of the mountain. We used them for cover. It was a mad, helter-skelter dash, laughing like schoolchildren toward the assembly area. Demhat, the German, is a man I can trust. There was a point, lying there in the rain against the cold earth in soaked clothes where we looked at each other's muddy faces. Our blue eyes met, & we laughed a stifled laugh uncontrollably for minutes. I do not know why. I do know that it was the most honest & the brightest laughter I can remember laughing for a very long time. Today was the best day since I toured the streets of Prague with Jim. Wish I'd written that one down too. It strikes me that in this journal I wrote none of our time together. Maybe I was too in the moments with my oldest & most cherished friend. Maybe I should spend more of my time cherishing these moments here. One day I will miss it. & the hurt will never fade. All that will be left are the relivings of these times in the rain, in the mud, laughing.*

Warren Stoddard II

Palmyra

I had a life here long before they came for the faces. I would wander out from the market stalls on early summer mornings before the sun broke entirely free of the ring of dust that rims the horizon, enjoying the morning air before the heat of the day, stopping to rest at the foot of an ancient column, leaning against antiquity. Life is old here. Unfortunately, in our time, it is also cheap.

This town has always survived on what it once was. People from around the world who otherwise might have never considered Syria an important place would somehow make their way here. I have seen men from Japan take photographs with their families under those fabled archways. Women from Germany, their blonde hair shining in our great sun, smiled from the stage of the theater. *On my eyes,* this place was once a crown jewel to the world. Now I cannot bear to look at it.

It was my wife who warned me. "They say they're over the hills," she said, she had a jug of sunflower oil in her hand. The sun on the baked earth out the doorway behind her ringed her in a halo of light.

"Who is they?"

"Which one?"

No matter how urgent a situation, she could find a way under my skin, I loved her for it. I smiled. “Who told you?”

“Latif. He says his cousin has come from Deir ez-Zor. He says months ago that Daesh came. They began to attack, they’ve destroyed the Armenian Church, but their gains in the city are not enough. They want to cut Deir ez-Zor off from west of the river.”

“Why would they come for us? All we have here are a few Roman rocks. We are in the middle of the desert.”

“Salim,” she said, setting the jug of oil in the entryway. She stepped forward and grabbed my hand, and her face, ringed by her blue hijab, pleaded with me, “Latif’s cousin says he was stopped at two checkpoints. They demanded ransom both times. He is now destitute. He says anyone who can should go for Damascus.”

“We’ll not go for Damascus,” I snapped. “Tadmor, Palmyra is our home. We cannot just leave it. Our parents, theirs before them, and so on, all lived and died here—traders, goatherds, working the ruins. This is our way of life. We cannot simply give it up and make for Damascus,” I spat the word. Damascus. “What will we find there, a cardboard box to live in? We have no family in Damascus.”

“Salim, they are going to come for us.”

“Why would they do such a thing?”

“They come for everyone; they want to cut of Deir ez-Zor” she said.

“It doesn’t matter,” I said. “We cannot simply make for Damascus. This is our home. What would we say one day, were God to bless us with a son? That we ran, like cowards? That we abandoned our home?"

"Oh, and what are you going to do, Salim? Are you going to take them on all by yourself? You cannot hardly see the houses opposite ours on the street. You are no fighter." She flung her hand at the old Kalashnikov propped up in the corner of the room. "You'd be lucky if you even shot it in the right direction."

I sat down on the sofa, leaning my back against the wall. Looking up at her I could see that she knew she had hurt me. I pulled off my glasses and rubbed my eyes and sighed. I did not look up at her again. "We will not leave," I said. "If Daesh come, they will soon see that our city is of no strategic value, they'll leave, and we can still go about our lives. In our home."

She said nothing to me. She stormed off, leaving me on the sofa, watching the drapery flutter about the doorframe. The ground outside shone harshly under the sun as an over-developed photograph. We ate dinner in silence.

It did not take them long at all. The next day, we saw their trucks—Toyota Hilux pickups with huge machineguns mounted to the beds, men clinging to them as the trucks drove, hollering wildly, and their black flag waving in the sun. Far away, blurred.

I was in the market, and as the first truck came into view across the ruins, silence fell over the whole place. By fear, the smells of the spices were stifled in the air so that all you could smell was the nothingness of sand and the pungent perfume of their exhaust. Latif was beside me, "Fuck them, we should have made for Damascus," he said, and I stared at him gravely. In the eyes looking back at me I believe I could see he wanted some commiseration from me, some common defiance, but I only wanted to be left alone, I only wanted to sell my trinkets to whatever tourists trickled into the Roman ruins, and to see foreigners smiling in the theater. Syria had been at war for four years; I wanted to will it away, to pretend that it did not happen, as people in the west can pretend calamity does not befall them and continue on in their happy lives, but the war only inched closer. I wanted to sell my wares to the tourists and walk the ruins and wonder how men so long ago could create all this from nothing while we now only watched cities burn to nothing on the news.

I could hear shrieking coming from the outskirts of the city, and I turned and ran, juking and bounding between spice stalls and stunned shoppers, sprinting along the dusty streets home. Eva met me at the door, flinging her arms around me.

"We have to leave," she cried, tugging at my shirt.

"No, no, no, no, we will be fine. It will be okay. I promise you. They won't hurt us; we are good Muslims." But no matter how I tried to console her, she only sobbed into my chest, pounding at me with her fists. I led her indoors, bolting the door shut and drawing the drapes across all the windows. I took the Kalashnikov from the corner and held it in my hands, not knowing what to do with it. "I have to get rid of this," I said. And I could just see the irises of her eyes shatter like dropped tableware.

I removed the dust cover, tucked it beneath the sofa, the magazine was stashed in a teapot, the bolt I blended in with the kitchen utensils, and the body of the rifle was crammed into a crevice in the rafters of the low ceiling of our house. "We cannot let them think we are the enemy," I said.

"We have to leave."

"No."

"We must make for Damascus. We have to go. We have to go to Damascus, Jordan, anywhere, we have to get out of here, Salim."

And I reached back my hand and slapped her. I felt the sting of it on my palm, could see the red of her cheek in the dim light on the sofa. "Be quiet," I said. "They will not hurt us, there is nothing for them in Palmyra but ruins, nothing in Tadmor but a spice market. They will see that, and they will go, and we will be fine."

Eva sat in stunned silence on the sofa, feeling the sting of her cheek, vigorously working at a set of worry beads she pulled from the tea table. I could hear their trucks groaning down the street outside.

Other doors were banged on. Muffled shouts echoed off my own floors and roof. What could they want here? What could they want with this dried up desert outpost? We were nothing but a tourist attraction before the war, now we are just a dusty outcropping of houses in the middle of the desert on the road to Deir ez-Zor. I shut my eyes and tried with everything that I could to will it away and be back among the columns in the ruins watching the sun glint off of blonde hair in the theater. I could hear the thuds and the shouts still coming down the street with the sound of the engine, and then they were outside my own door. And I opened my eyes to see the door bolt shatter and the door be flung open by a man in black, his face covered by a thin scarf. His eyes were bare, angry. He pointed his rifle at me.

"Get up," he said.

I stood.

"Make the bitch come too."

I turned around, I motioned for Eva to stand and come with me, and we walked out into the sunlight. They made us follow the procession already on its way to the ruins. Old neighbors and friends with stunned eyes shambled meekly through our streets. The black-clad men watched from the rooftops. They hoisted their black flag with its words painted white: "There is no god but God. Mohammad is the messenger of God." I believed in these words too; why had they come for me? Why had they ripped me from my home?

We filed through Palmyra, we wound our way through the columns, and in the distance, we could hear explosions in the museum building where the statues were housed. They were destroying the faces. The ancient faces. Iconoclasts. What had the faces done to them?

And then we were at the theater, stepping down the steps to the stage at its base, the rocks of the seats and the steps hewn from our very earth, sitting stout as a testament to something great that once reigned, before falling. Now falling again. More rumbling and shattering brick could be heard above us, and I knew that it was the arches. In our time, buildings only fall.

Once we were gathered on the stage of the theater, men in black ringed the seats around us, rifles ready, their stares cold and impersonal, as if they were watching the slaughter of a goat for the Eid. As if we were something to be got out of the way before a great celebration.

"People," a man spoke, a great beard bobbing from his chin with each syllable. "Congratulations are in order; we have liberated you."

"Allahu akbar!" came the shouts of the men around him. They thrust the barrels of their rifles into the air.

Glory to God. And liberated from what?

"You are now free of your fettered existence, and you are citizens of the great Caliphate–The Islamic State!" He paused as if he expected us to cheer, but there were only frightened stares of discontent in response. "As members of this great Caliphate," he went on, "we can offer you a great many things. Men, those of you who are able-bodied will be offered the chance to fight alongside us, in the name of God, in the tradition of the great prophet Muhammad."

I could hear quiet murmurs around me, skittish at this proposition, boys too young to become men, grandfathers with arms too tired to lift a rifle.

"And women, you who are unmarried will find great seats beside us, you will cook for our fighters, you will be sure his needs are met, and if you are lucky, you will be granted a child, to further along our pure Caliphate. But purity," he went on, pausing, clearing his throat, his beard shaking, his wild eyes catching the sun, "purity must begin here."

Around me, people began to fidget uncomfortably, as if they were seeking an avenue of escape, but there was nowhere to run. And I suddenly became aware of the black-clad men's fingers resting on the triggers of their rifles, all switched off safe, ready to fire at the slightest provocation.

"Now surely there are those among you who have waited all your lives to become great defenders of God. Step forward now."

Beside me, some young men stepped forward, their eyes wide. The speaker caught the attention of a boy no more than sixteen. "You," he said, "tell me, who are the infidels? Which of your neighbors is a disgrace to the name of God? Where are the Christians, the Jews, the atheists, the sodomites; who among your neighbors is *haram*?"

At first, the boy was too startled to speak.

"Come here my son," the man said. And he coaxed him up the stairs. He whispered something into his ear, and be boy looked down to the ground and nodded. The man lifted his chin with a finger. He looked into his eyes. "You know these people. Now tell me, who are the infidels?"

And the boy began to point.

The black-clad men stepped down from the stairs and they began pulling people from the crowd. Women were shrieking, trying to cling to the arms of their husbands. The men were resisting, writhing against the arms of their captors, trying vainly to free themselves. Three gunshots rang out. And as the echoes died against the ancient stairs of the amphitheater, the desert went silent. Two bodies lay on the ground, their faces buried in the sand, blood pooling beside them. The rest of the crowd the boy had pointed out were led up the stairs with their hands bound by zip ties.

The man spoke again: "I am glad we have purified you, after having so graciously liberated you only today. To remain pure, to keep close to His holy commandments, some things will change. The name of this old city, Palmyra, is *haram*, it is offensive to our God, it venerates pagans, nonbelievers, the *kafir*. We will destroy the rest of these old ruins for you. You will not have to worry about further offending God."

But I was a good Muslim, how could my life have offended God? What God is so fragile as to take offense at the name of an old city, at the stone faces of statues? Their god could not be my God, but their flags said it, but they had killed—quickly—without remorse—the bodies were still lying on the sand. Who were these men? What kind of Muslims?

"Women," the man continued, now sitting on a step cockily, resting an elbow on his knee, "I am pleased to inform those of you unmarried that you are now given the privilege of joining our harem. Congratulations."

I could see the tendons of my wife's cheek tensing in rage. Eyes burning bright with fiery hatred.

"And all of you, married or not, will wear the niqab. Your hijabs are *haram* too. Your faces are only for your husband. To parade about town with your lips and eyes for all the world to see is *pornographic*, and it will not be tolerated."

"No."

You could almost hear the eyes in the amphitheater lance toward the sound; feet shuffled, heads swiveled toward who had said it. And I was stunned to hear it just over my left shoulder. And I winced as she spoke again.

"No."

I couldn't bear to look at her. My eyes were paralyzed with fright. What if they came for me too? What if they had seen me look to her and came for me as well?

Two men leapt from the seats of the stadium, bullying their way through the crowd of people on the stage. In the jostling you could hear gunshots ring out in the old city far above us, you could hear more detonations, more pillars and arches crumbling, more faces being blown from rock, and I could hear my wife shrieking as the men grabbed her by her arms. I could not look at her, but I could feel the men stumble back into me as she kicked at them. I could hear her teeth biting into flesh, and I could hear a fist crush her rib, and I could feel her knees give out beneath her, I could feel her sink as she was dragged by her scalp out in front of the crowd. I could feel her knees on the rough sand as the man stepped down from the seats, his boots slapping with finality at the ground.

"Is that so?" he said. And standing before her, he turned, a shamshir was offered to him, and I could feel his rough palms against the polished wooden hilt of the blade as he lifted it, "what a pity. I would have loved to take you into my bed." I knew she was beaten, I knew she hung there held by the shoulders by two men in black uniforms, but I could not look. I heard the whistle of the sword as it was raised into the sky, and the reflection of the sun off the steel caught my eye, and I looked up to see the curved blade come down with another whistle, her neck offering no resistance. And I saw her head rolling away from her body, her eyelids weakly holding open, her cheek still red from where I had slapped her.

And now months later, I walk these streets under their flag, these streets that were once called Palmyra, now known only as Tadmor, they are still as dusty as they were in my childhood, but the ruins on the hill are more rubble than testament to anything. A stone lies where it does. And in the market, trading spices, selling trinkets to any of the new soldiers in town, I can feel the eyes of my neighbors on me, calling me coward, asking me why did I not run, why did I not flee to Damascus, why did I not try to save her, why did I not die in her stead? But Daesh have taken everything from me. How could I let them take my home as well?

19 November 2018: Dêrik, Rojava:

The women's wails echoed off the walls of the morgue as though the simple act of singing the song amplified itself. Baran, Şoreş, & Zafer were on one side of the coffin; Rêdûr, Haqî, & I were on the other. It was wrapped in paper like a present–that coffin; red & gold & green with flowers of the same & a Styrofoam dove the lone burst of white atop the lid. We hoisted it. & the heft of Şahîn's body was heavy as we made our way through the doors & into the light outside. To our left & right were throngs of people. Some civilians, some doctors, some soldiers in camouflage with wallet-sized pictures of Şehîd Şahîn Qereçox pinned to their breast pockets. "Şehîd na mirin!" they chanted. Martyrs never die. Video cameras swarmed the scene like hornets buzzing in & out between the people. We laid the coffin in the rear of a hearse. Soro & Çîya climbed in back with me. The crowd all piled into cars & overloaded beds of pickup trucks with YPG & Rojava flags fluttering from open windows. Driving through Dêrik, the shoulders of the road were lined with hundreds–thousands of people. As we passed, those people too hopped in cars & trucks & joined the procession that must have stretched some two miles behind us as we rounded Mount Qereçox headed for the Sêmalka border crossing. In every small village the scene from Dêrik repeated itself. School children, workers, & young cowards of our own age too craven to fight for their own country watched as the body of a young man from France was driven past them. Everyone flashed the victory sign. My friend lays there in that hearse with me with half his skull cleared away by shrapnel. He lies there dead for a country that was not his & he is happy. The children of the world will ensure victory for this land. We will help shoulder the load. At Sêmalka we heard speeches from Baran & Ciwan, saw drill & ceremony, & felt the heat of the sun warm us from a chill draught under a blue sky of uniform cauliflower shade from Başûr to Rojava; Iraq to Syria. If the world does not pay, then the price of victory cannot be met. Şahîn's body was given to his family at the border to return to France—his "homeland." His soul remains here. His blood, which stained this corner of the earth, will sow the seeds of victory.

Warren Stoddard II

The Trial of Heval Firas

We had a fascist in our midst. I know, I know, I know, I know. *I know*—how could we have let this happen? Let's be honest here. It couldn't have been too difficult for him to infiltrate us. Just fill out a questionnaire, answer what you believe they want to hear. Buy a plane ticket, and boom, there you are in Syria to fight ISIS. And he *was* there to fight ISIS, or anyone really. This fucker—Firas—was crazy as shit.

The night he turned up, sometime after midnight, he seemed relatively unassuming: an Italian, short, stout, thick, heavy glasses rimming his eyes like basketball hoops. His English wasn't very good, but there were enough bilingual Italians around to translate for him when necessary, and he had plenty of time to brush up on it or learn Kurdish.

But after a little while, some things began to seem off. Stories started to surface. Whispers. "Man, I'm telling you, when we were on the way over here, in the mountains, he was telling us he couldn't wait to get to Rojava to rape and pillage liberated ISIS villages."

"Ok, that seems like it was a joke to me." And besides, the man telling me this, Alîşer, looked like a fucking Looney Tune. Short, red-haired, and wiry, his glasses looked like

Jeffrey Dahmer's, and he was constantly espousing some sort of drama or other, yelling over non-vegetarian dinner options, or quietly doing yoga poses on his own, telling us he couldn't wait to get his first knife kill. And he carried a big one—one to put Jim Bowie to shame—it never left his side.

But then Firas began to sing songs in the showers, they would echo off the tile walls of the little building and out into the air in Italian. They were translated to us English speakers. "I wipe my ass with the red flag." Audible gasps were heard from those around me, and I could see more than one hammer and sickle from where I sat. It wasn't going to go over well. When the singing was brought up to him, Firas balked.

"No, I was just singing a song from my village in Sicily. My father sang this one to me." He spoke with his lower jaw waving about wildly. His eyes simply not understanding.

"You know that you've come to Syria to join an anti-fascist militia, right? And many of us are socialists or communists. This isn't okay."

"What is wrong with fascism?"

We planted our faces in our hands. "You've got to be kidding me."

"What? It gets a bad name for no reason. What is so wrong with fascism? The socialists are the ones who beat Mussolini to death and hung him upside down."

"Because Mussolini was a fascist. He sent people to death camps."

Firas looked like a god-damned Neanderthal. He held his palms up toward the sky and widened his eyes as though he did not understand.

And then the rumors began to fly. Mostly from Alîşer. "He was saying he wanted to fuck YPJ when we were in the mountains. He pointed to one while her back was turned and started thrusting his hips. He's a rapist."

When he was confronted about this, he simply turned his palms up toward the sky again, "No? I would never do that."

And so we could do nothing. His only saving grace was that the man could cook, which is a rarity among the lunatics who venture to Syria to fight with the YPG. "Hell, if we can keep him around long enough to get his recipes, that'll be alright by me."

"No, I'm taking this fucker down," Alîşer said. And so he began laying traps. He'd leave his phone beside Firas' bed to record his conversations. He'd wander around the base, talking to whoever would listen about the many sins of Heval Firas: "He wasn't in the Italian Special Forces. He's just a paratrooper. He said if we went to Afrin to fight the Turks and we started to lose, that he would jump to their side. I've heard him talking about all the great things Mussolini did for Italy."

And so on. In the beginning, we rolled our eyes, wanting it all to smooth over, but then our pet praying mantis, Nimej, came up missing a leg. He was Alîşer's prize camel-spider-killer. He carried the little bug around for weeks, doting on him, giving him water from a wet cloth, feeding him spiders and scorpions. Firas hated it, and he kept trying to find other insects that could defeat it. The gladiator-style matches happened nightly—Nimej the winner by KO every time. A litter of discarded legs laying in his home like throwaway chicken bones.

And then we heard the screaming and ran to the source of it.

"Where the fuck is he?"

Firas looked to all of us as we entered the room, "Get this man off of me. He is crazy!"

"Tell me what the fuck you did with Nimej."

He turned his palms toward the sky as if he did not know.

"Where the fuck is Nimej?"

Gone. No one could get the answer out of him, but no one spoke to Firas as a friend again. We all hated him now. More people and more people among our number began to record their conversations with the Italian, and he began to move in the shadows. Alîşer shifted his knife to the front of his belt.

"If that fucker comes at me, I'm gonna stab him in the neck."

And in the shower one day, where Alîşer was known to sometimes sit on the tile floor and meditate, Firas beat violently on the metal door, screaming bloody murder in Italian, and then he ran away in a showertime version of ding-dong-ditch.

Alîşer emerged, wide-eyed, his knife drawn and face taut, looking like a pint-sized Irish Rambo, dripping water. He looked me dead in the eye, "We need to kill that fucker."

I'd tried the best I could to continue to smooth things over, but it was gone too far now, and we went to the commanders with our complaints.

"Heval," they said, "You cannot just kick someone out of the YPG because you do not like them, they have to do something, some crime actually, or so on and so forth."

The whispers continued to swirl, and his conversations continued to be taped. Late one night, I felt a hand pulling my foot. I looked up, "What is it?" I asked.

"I need you to listen to something. You speak Spanish, no?"

"Sí," I said.

He played me a taped conversation between him and Firas.

"I hate these fuckers," Firas said in Spanish.

"Why do you hate them?"

"They treat me like a second-class citizen, and everything is blamed on me, and I know they all talk about me behind my back. And Alîşer, he is no good. This man, he is bad. He has been out to get me since day one. I hate him."

"Are you going to do anything? Or can you work it out?"

"I want to take his big knife and stab him. Or I will call the American FBI and get him into big trouble. No, I will sneak into the room of Azad, I will take his rifle and his bullets, and I will shoot Alîşer, and anyone who tries to stop me I will shoot too." He laughed—maniacally, like some shitty Disney villain. I swear I pictured him as Ursula from *The*

Little Mermaid. But my rifle was the only one with live ammunition in it, the rest were only training dummies.

"This motherfucker."

"Speak to the commanders with me tomorrow?"

We went to them. We played them the tape. And they nodded gravely.

"This is a very serious accusation, heval."

"It was a very serious threat."

They had me come with them to his room, a round chambered in my rifle. "If he moves to make attack to you, you can kill, heval," but he went without much of a fight, a sole whimper maybe, his palms turned up toward the sky as if he did not understand.

We kept him locked away in a bedroom for a few days. We fed him what we ate, and he was allowed to leave to go to the bathroom, but only under the eyes of an armed guard. At night, guard duty shifts were spent on the roof opposite his room staring with intent into his window, watching his silhouette pace about behind the curtain, seeing his hand draw the curtain away to look out into the night, then let it sway shut again.

He was put on trial on a sunny day in September. His palms never turned away from the sky as we read our accusations to him, our criticisms, and what we believed should be his punishment. He made as if he understood none of it, even with the Italian translation, and cocked his head in a feigned effort to understand random sentences we spoke or accusations we hurled.

In the end, it came down to a vote. After all of our complaints, accusations, criticisms, and recommendations were heard, the commanders had us raise our hands. "Now, who votes that he should remain in Rojava, write a report, and be given the opportunity to change his ways?" Not a hand stirred. "Temam. Who then wishes for him to be removed from Rojava, we take him to the Iraqi border, and we leave him there with cab fare to get to a city with an airport? He can never come to here again." Hands were practically flying up like fish caught in a tornado, flapping about, jumping about, begging for all this to be at end, all but one. "Temam, and who wishes for us to take him to 'the river?' You know, we 'send him to Paris' we take him to 'the grand river in the sky'?" Firas' palms were turned upwards as if he did not understand again, and Alîşer's hand was stout, immovably erect, pointed to the ceiling with resolve and determination.

His eyes were glowing crazily, his knife quivering in its sheath, his glasses reflecting Firas' confused look. "Kill that fascist motherfucker."

20 December 2018: Qereçox, Rojava: Noktaya Şehîd Kendal Breizh:

"If you would just let us watch movies, we wouldn't have to watch porn!" – Soro, during a short-lived ban on cable television.

A laid-back day. Lessons began late, & after Kurmanji classes we ran stressed medical drills with fire & yelling under the courtyard roof. The rain fell heavy outside. Both streams are surging powerfully with turbid water. In the afternoon, we went over the Biksî; I am warming up to the idea of using the weapon. It is a bad fucking gun. The mechanical side of it is like home to me; the extra weight is the only hang up. Most of the world news today has been dominated by the United States'—Donald Trump's—decision to withdraw from Syria. Our abandonment. The orange idiot says ISIS is defeated when we are still engaged in heavy fighting to the south in Hajin. Before Trump made the decision, he apparently had extensive conversations with Turkish President Erdoğan. Fucking scumbags. So much for the Kurdish sacrifice in the fight against Daesh—still not fully finished. So much for "our Kurdish brothers." So much for American credibility & trust-worthiness. They will find no friends in the Middle East now. France will stay; maybe that can deter the Turks, but I doubt it. Demonstrations against the move were held across Rojava today. Watching them made my blood boil, made me yearn to fight. Let them come. I hate that I have become so tired of life here at this moment. To leave feels like abandoning the cause & my friends to die. Just as my country now plans to do.

But to stay without any major change feels like a death knell for my sanity & suicide for myself. No one here can honestly say that they are not afraid to fight Turkey with no help. Just look to what happened in Afrin. But we hate them as much as we hate ISIS, because they are one in the same. I do not know what to do once again. My head tells me to go when my 6 months is finished in 5 days—you must look after yourself. Is there any glory in certain death? All death is certain. My heart is torn. To go home, to love, to live freely again, to stay & resist, to fight with my brothers against impossible odds. Nothing can ever be an easy decision. Look to the short term. The short term. This (hopefully still) upcoming operation is foremost in my mind. The last push to finish ISIS. I want the fight. Only once it is had can I consider peace.

Warren Stoddard II

A Good Place on the Banks of the Euphrates

My heart is hammering through my shirt and against the floor of the desert. The kickback of my rifle stirs up the dirt beneath me and dust clouds my vision, and the water flowing behind me is barely audible over the cacophony of war—the yelling—the small arms fire—I am yelling too, but I do not know what words or sounds I make. I am only aware of the squeeze of my finger against the trigger of my rifle—and the dust—and the hammering of my heart. That sound of flowing water behind me ekes itself into my conscience every so often to remind me that I am still human.

The squeezes of the trigger are more rapid now. They are getting closer. "They" of course is the enemy—that dehumanizing word that divides us and turns blood to confetti and trumpet celebrations. I see the faint pink mist of it when my squeezes find their target. A victory parade. I smile. It is not a common smile, but one that I imagine the Vikings made when they pillaged and plundered.

But I am on the side of the good. That is why I am here—for freedom, and liberty, and the rights of all men to live unperturbed. To give these downtrodden people a voice in this world. To let them raise their own banner. I am surely on the side of the good. But I wonder if the Vikings thought the same thoughts.

We men have not evolved much, women either, for that matter; they fight beside me as well. Their war cries mix in with that unbearable silence from the rifles and the yelling and the ringing of the ears. How long have we fought this way? Was the ringing there in the ears of those who did battle with swords and axes? Perhaps the ringing of the ears is a defense mechanism to prevent you from losing your humanity—that viral breakdown of your spirit can only enter through the ears I am told by the devil-tongued masters of lies—those philosophers and overthinkers corrupt who we are. Of course, that itself is a lie—only man can corrupt himself. The ringing must be there to block it all out. At least in this way your memory will not be able to bring up the full extent of those auditory horrors you endured.

Distinctly, oddly enough in all this, I vehemently know that memory must end someday. I fear it, somewhere in the periphery.

And there it is, faintly. That one that I have been awaiting for so long. It is far off and begins slow and quiet.

And I am squeezing the trigger of my rifle.

And the dust is in my eyes.

And I can faintly feel the sound of the water sliding along the banks pushing itself into my conscience.

And then it meets an opposition—ever the slightest nudge in the opposite direction. What I have been awaiting has reached its destination. The sound of the water is swept away by a heaviness that I cannot feel upon me, but it is somewhere within me, and it begins to drag me down.

I try to squeeze my trigger, but I cannot.

The yelling is now caught in my vocal cords, and it cannot escape.

The dust is in my eyes, but they are dimming, and I am trying to fight it off in the manner of how I may curb drowsiness, but when the hypnic jerk should come, there is only the weight, and now the faint pink is all in the sky, and it is like watching the most beautiful sunset—the ones where the sun shows its majesty and that power of the cosmos that we men have spent eons trying to sort.

And I fight to keep the vision from going dark, trying to take the gift of the world in just a bit longer before the weight takes me. The pressure within. The green banks of the river downstream. The blue of the sky behind that sheer curtain of rose. The water behind me moving silently now. The grain of the wooden stock of the rifle. The cool smell of the metal. My dirty hands. I wish I could hear the ringing still. And the heaviness builds within.

Then the weight pulls me through as though I had fallen from a great height into a pane of thick glass that held the darkness at bay. The shards are all around me now like stars in the night sky. As I descend, the shards stay where they were when I went through the pane.

And I am falling now. And all around me is the blackness—above, below, beside, behind—emptiness. I am hurtling through it, but the only reference I have is that point from where I came far above. Receding—receding—receding. On the other side of the point is the blue of the sky, and as I fall further it becomes nothing but a tiny pinpoint of light. First the shards glimmer in it, and then I am too far gone to make them out, and there is nothing but that singular point of light now in my view, far above me. I am still hurtling through the darkness. It is emptiness too. All except for that white dot from where I sprung. I fall faster—faster—faster, and I think I may never reach terminal velocity, and I won't.

I am falling for a long, long time. For so long, but the pinpoint of light cannot get any smaller now. I am hurtling through a void of nonexistence. But a void is empty. And nothingness contains nothing. But *I* am here, and I make up my mind in this moment to stop falling—and that's just what I do. I simply stop, and then I decide to stand, so I do. And I am standing on nothing and surrounded by nothing with nothing to do and nowhere to be, and I feel something clinch within me. A contraction of dread.

I know why I have come, but the admission would make it far too real for me, so I look up, and far, far, impossibly far above me is still that pinpoint of light—like the night had been wiped completely clean except for one star at the zenith. I close my eyes, and it disappears. I reopen them, see it again. I yell. There is no echo. The sound is dead as soon as it escapes my lips. It might as well have been silent.

My knees fail me, and I am falling again. I stop myself once more and decide to sit. And I am sitting there in this emptiness for a long time. I do not know if it has been an hour or a decade, and there suddenly I realize that I am not sitting alone. You are there, and I am glad for it. It has been such a long time since we have seen each other, but I know I cannot look—not until I decide that it is true.

We sit there a while like two old friends on the bank of a river. I do not look up to see the point of light, only straight in front of me. After a time, I speak.

"Do you ever get used to it?"

I hear your voice again. "I think you already have."

"It isn't so bad," I say. But I know I miss the flowing of the water, and the blue of the sky, even the cacophony. I miss the smell of white roses. The ones I found in your garden.

That emptiness stretches infinitely before us. So we decide to stand, and we take a walk together and after a while we sit on that bank again. We have not spoken in ages it seems. But then I am speaking to you now, and we laugh together, and we do toasts to our good fortune. In a happy stupor, I slur, "What the hell is this place?"

You are there somewhere outside of my peripherals, and you smile and laugh and say, "Why don't you tell me?" So I do.

We laugh again, and it is like I am sitting at your table once more, though now it is in the shade of a tree, on the grass, on the edge of the nothingness. A river.

And we smile that crooked smile together—the one where you have found something that you thought you might have forgot.

And we realize that we are not just the two of us anymore.

And there is laughter all around us, and I make my way through the crowd and hear the greetings of long gone away friends and smell the roses on the tables. The burbling of conversation warms my ear. I go to the other side of the tree from the table where we sat, and I look up for the first time since we were sitting on these banks together and see that the space far above me from where I came is overcrowded with a galaxy of little pinpoints of light, and I smile, and I can hear that sound of flowing water sliding along the banks.

21 December 2018: Qereçox, Rojava, Noktaya Şehîd Kendal Breizh:

Welcome to the front. We are now less than 10 miles from a hostile enemy force kitted out with the best equipment NATO money can buy. Mattis has resigned in a protest of Trump's decision—at least he was a true friend to us & our cause; now we have little left but one another... & the mountains. News rains in from dozens of perspectives & often gives conflicting stories:

The SDF has pulled out of the Hajin pocket/SDF will pull out if Turkey attacks.

Regime & Iran massing troops to take over ISIS fight in Deir ez-Zor/Regime massing troops for an assault on the Autonomous Administration of Northeast Syria.

Turkey may attack within days/Turkey will hold off on operations until US withdrawal is complete.

Regime not interested in talks with SDF/SDF & Regime reach deal on Qami şlo oil fields & border protection.

"May you live in interesting times" - ancient Chinese curse.

Little is certain, but now I am the machine gunner—Biksîci. Nûbar is my A-gunner. I love that weapon. The power one feels watching rounds tear downrange is immense & indescribable, as if a freight train were being unleashed at your will. I hope I get the chance to use it—on Daesh (if the SDF is still in the Hajin pocket & operations will still happen) or on the Turks if they begin to pour over that line to the north. They are watching us; this much is certain. You can hear the low baritone hum of the drones circling over us. & we are in the shadow of Mt. Qereçox—a place airstruck by the Turks only 2 years ago. They are up there prowling like sharks, moving like mechanized doom. There is no defense against the drones but luck; no skill can save you from them if & when they decide you are a target. We have taken our pennants down, the flags furled & put away. We have lost Agît to the desires of home. As he says, "In times of war, any hole is a trench." & we talk of little but impending destruction, & we laugh about it. So long as we have our friends, we will all be ok. If our comrades are beside us, we will be alright, no matter what comes our way.

The International Tabûr, September 2018

Left: Killing kitchen flies, July 2018

Below: Martial arts training, July 2018

Planting the garden, July 2018

On nobet, August 2018

Right: Flag burning, August 2018

Below: The aftermath of an intra-YPG soccer match, September 2018

Above: Movement training, October 2018

Left: Puppies, October 2018

Above: The November funeral of French volunteer Şahîn Qereçox, killed in action in Deir ez-Zor in October, 2018
Right: Şehîd Şahîn Qereçox
(YPG Press Office)

The Syrian countryside, Siwêdîk village on the hill,
December 2018

Left: Trying out a welding mask, December 2018

Right: Şehîd Hîwa Bosko, who killed himself in December 2018 (YPG Press Office)

Above: Kurdish lessons, December 2018

Below: Loading the truck for operations.
Hajin, Syria, January 2019

The front line in Hajin, January 2019

Left: Arab QSD fighters, January 2019

Below: The ruins of Hajin seen through a killhole, January 2019

Airstrike in Ash Sha'fah,
January 2019

Plane, landed. February 2019

Photo by Bob Miller for the *New York Times*

Warren Stoddard II

Viva la Quince Brigada

Had this been Spain would the air in the night in winter have smelled any different? Powdered dust still hangs on a crisp breeze. Phosphorous haze still pricks the inside of the nose like a needle. And gunpowder is still as pungent in Syria as in Spain. There is shit down the stairwell. Dried blood on uniforms is earthen–metallic. The smell always takes you back. You could recall, as a little boy, the stainless-steel scent of blood, being fascinated watching the bandage grow red as the blood seeped through as now one watches night seep into the day, watches a flare hang stubbornly in the sky over a file of men walking through the crimson glow into darkness.

You filed down the stairs onto the street after them, careful to avoid the pile of shit. And down on the street under the palm fronds in the night with the flare dropping between the hamlets in the next little village, giving darkness back to its possessor, you turned to us. "So this is the war," you said, though you had seen it before. But you knew then what we did not in that every war is different, and every war is the same. And then you plucked a hard-boiled egg from a carton at the edge of the asphalt, plucked an orange from another, peeled the shell from the egg and the rind from the orange and dropped the flakes to the ground so that they alternated orange white orange white orange white. And you ate. We all ate there beside the road in the cold listening to the idling of a Humvee and conversations in Arabic we did not understand.

"I wish there were some Kurds here. I don't know what the fuck's going on." Because you speak no Arabic, and neither do the rest of us.

And in Spain, what did they think? What did they think some eighty years prior? Our forefathers. What did those young American and British and French and Irish and Cypriot and Greek and Polish young men think in the night in the dead of winter in Madrid or Guadalajara or Segovia? They were crouching in trenches and peeling oranges and eggs, eating as they peeled and allowing the crumbs and the juices to drop from their mouths to the pile of white shell and orange rind in the dirt. There were fascist forces across the valley, and they wished there were Spaniards beside them now instead of Poles or Cypriots or Frenchmen.

"Do you know what time we'll move out?"

"Judging by the food? Soon."

And they would have known what they were to do, for it was always to move west as it is for you and I to move south. And they would move west to take some strategic bunker with a panoramic view of the countryside so that some Russian general or Catalan general could whip a tear in a tabled map with his riding crop and declare that the taking of this bunker would be a decisive gain for the offensive. But the men in the trench would not know. They hardly knew what Spain was.

But they had come in the thousands to answer the call that their countries would not—the Abraham Lincoln Brigade, the Sixth of February Battalion, the André Marty Battalion, and many others went just as we had come in droves to defend this land we had never seen simply because *it was the right thing to do*. All those before us joined together on the side of the fledgling Spanish Republic against Franco and his fascist state sponsors—Italy, Nazi Germany. And those fascists were just across the valley from the trench, as ours are across the night, black-clad with black flags.

"It is time to go," one of them said in the trench, and men stood up in the pitch blackness. In the night outside they checked their pockets and belts for grenades and bayonets. Their rifles were old, dilapidated relics left over from the first world war. Few even used the same ammunition as another. And away under a starless sky they crouched and moved slowly through the valley and then up the hill. Among them, Eric Blair's canteen rattled sharply, and the group of them stopped. But perhaps we there in Syria knew him better as George Orwell.

We had all read his books, his *Homage to Catalonia*, and in it he had told us that "However much one cursed at the time, one realized afterwards that one had been in contact with something strange and valuable." And I was thinking of it then, as we climbed onto the roof of the Humvee and rolled away under the red light of the flare, trying to leave Robert Jordan's pine-needled floor of the forest for another day, trying to ignore my heart beating against the inside of my vest, the stock of my rifle jammed against my shoulder, the safety off.

You could hear them, in Spain, as they each clicked their rifles to fire, but at the crest of the hill the fascists were enjoying a campfire, they were talking calmly, laughing about something boisterously enough to make the silhouette against the cloud-covered moon seem almost a person, and those men climbing the hill could hear the redeeming qualities of humanity be poured into the silhouette, but they kept moving, splitting into two groups now, one moving to the left a ways and stopping below the crest of the hill, the other group crawling to the right and vanishing over the top, out of sight. The night was quiet. And those men waiting in still shadows could feel the cold of their feet biting against the insides of their cracked boots as the right-hand group moved into position. Eyes silently watched watches and stowed them back into pockets.

The night was not so quiet for you and me. You could hear the road beneath the tires being churned into dust. Asphalt had been blown away by the jets, and those airstrikes still lacerated the night off in the distance. When their missiles hit, the sparks that showered from them would create silhouettes of the buildings of the city of Ash Sha'fah. You could see it from the roof of the Humvee, and you raised your night-vision goggles to your eyes and scanned about us as I peered back into the darkness wielding my M-16 as a child wields a flashlight in safeguard against the encroaching night.

The wheels lurched again, and you and I were almost thrown from the vehicle, but the rays of the headlights merely bounced about off the façades of the buildings we rolled past. My heart was hammering now, and though you looked so calm I knew yours was too, you could almost see it—the scar on your cheek from years prior when the enemy's round found its way in through your neck and out through the side of your mouth. "Fucking ISIS," you would say when you spoke of it, and you swore you would kill one this time. And the scar would clinch up. I knew you were chewing at the tissue on the inside of your cheek.

In the time of Spain such an injury would have killed you, but there were many among that number on the hillside that had been or would be wounded in the course of the war by fascist bullets or fascist shrapnel from fascist planes and they said "fucking fascists" so often when they spoke of their injuries that to hear them speak the word turned the two syllables into little more than a contemptuous spit from an alcoholic:

"You will never make me better. I am poisoned by hate, and I am proud."

They all were; there in the night fear became replaced by incipient rage that eventually blossomed into courage when the time came. And pride in the end. And as the watches were pulled from their pockets again, they looked about them, hardly seeing the whites of eyes in the darkness, but feeling the reciprocal look from their comrades. Hands went into pockets again, this time emerging with fists full of grenades.

My own grenades were clanging against the roof of the Humvee when another of our group tapped me on the shoulder from the turret of the vehicle. "Mines," he said. And I suppose I was meant to find some solace in knowing that the possibility of soon being launched from my perch had been upgraded to a likelihood, but I did not. But my heart did slow, and fear became replaced by incipient rage.

I could see them now. You could too—the faces. Faces of our martyred friends, their countenances immortally emblazoned over yellow backgrounds and green fields with red YPG and YPJ stars hanging in the top left like a medal on the chest of a man in a black and white photograph hidden away in a box. And we could see the faces of the old men now who never, *never under any circumstances* would lift the latch of that trunk and dig through the contents to find that photo and the one behind it, the one that had everyone in it, all dressed up, just before shipping out or being deployed or whatever preferable euphemism there is for going off to war to die screaming in dirt and heat alone in a far-off place where you and I and the old men could not save them, or to die right next to us as we bled from wounds minor by comparison. We could see the faces of the innocent, the faces of hanged children, and the faces of slaves. I am sure they saw the same ones in Spain.

And as incipient rage turned to courage in silence beneath the boughs in the cold Iberian darkness, the minute hand of the clock inched forward. Pins were pulled from grenades. Nods were exchanged. And in quickness the grenades were hurled over the crest of the hill, their pins flung into the darkness. And as the little orbs flew towards them, the fascists in the bunker could hear shouts of "¡No pasarán!" from down the hill—alarmingly close.

Then the night erupted.

Everything became a twisting and a turning and a hurling about for the fascists in the bunker. Heat sang off shrapnel as it flew through the air. Men screamed in agony when they were hit. Men screamed in fear when muzzle flashes burst the placid night to their left. The fascists struggled to return fire, whipping up K-98s as though they were moving through viscous syrup. Their ears rang. The cacophony became a deafening substitute for silence. Everything was muffled. The concussive bursts of grenades hit their chests, beat the water from their eyes. The actions of their rifles could not move quickly enough. Returning fire was laborious. Fear seeped in past the ringing of the ears, filling the head with it like embalming fluid. The fascists froze four at a time, looking about for confirmation from their peers but only finding further confusion. They could still hear the republicans' cries in the night as the second group crested the hill from the fascist front.

"¡No pasarán!"

"¡No pasarán!"

"¡No pasarán!" They shall not pass. And the fascists, in their final moments, considered what an odd battle cry it was for an attack. They considered what an odd shade of red the blood is when it is pooling from you and the moon emerges from behind wintry clouds. And then they were finished, and any redeeming qualities of humanity they might have held were lost and washed away as incipient rage turned to courage and back to hate and then the fear that left the remembrance of things for us. Those hated dead could never have been human now.

For to us the fascists were the enemy, that was their *natural place in the world.* You put it best, "They all deserve to die." But surely they could not have all been murderers and evil fiends. To some, something of value must have existed in their ways for them to win that war in Spain. But that victory was forgotten—overshadowed by the defeat of the Nazis, of Mussolini's pumpkined head, of horrors committed. And when that fascist victory was forgotten the power of it was too, and things that should not have been left alone were lost, left to fester on in brooding silence, anticipating, waiting for a spark to fall on dry tinder by the grace of the winds.

In irony, the spark was the later victor, sixty years on. American forces invaded Iraq in 2003 under pretext of ridding the Saddam regime of its weapons of mass destruction. And a generation of young Iraqi boys watched as heavily armed and armored white men battered the doors of their neighbors down, they watched as they stormed into their own homes, upsetting tea kettles and grabbing their fathers by the scruff of their neck *without even taking off their shoes*. And those young boys began to hate. And hate bred in a petri dish of violence turns to violence for power. So it should have come as no surprise when the Islamic State declared its Caliphate, when they became the heavily armed men bursting into Parisian theaters and storming the slopes of Mount Sinjar and locking hundreds of young Yazidi boys, as they had once been young, in their very own schoolhouses to spray them down with bullets as they sold their mothers and sisters into sex slavery. It should have shocked no one. It shocked the world. But it should have come as no surprise that they would exterminate "the other" as Americans once did, that they would retake the power in Mesopotamia in the same manner it was stripped from them—violently.

I could feel it burbling inside me now as the Humvee rounded a bend in the road. The walls beside us were hemming in, and I wished to god that one of them would jump out now. For no matter who created this mess, whoever struck the match, the only way to oppose fascism is to violently extinguish it like it were a rug on fire.

They had burned them. They had taken Christians and burned them alive in cages. They had taken journalists and burned them alive in cages. They had taken Kurds and burned them alive in cages. They had taken Syriacs and burned them alive in cages. Kill any who would threaten the homogeny, that was the only way for it to go on. So burn them. Alive.

And America had done nothing. Nothing.

I had seen the faces of young Kurds killed. I had seen the faces of young westerners killed too, fighting for a land that was not theirs but fighting because *it was the right thing to do.* Because if it happens on the other side of the world, it happens in your own back yard. Because if one person suffers the lot of humanity suffers under the same whip. Because a threat to justice anywhere is a threat to justice everywhere. Because any man's death diminishes me. Because I am a part of *mankind.* And because of Hemingway and because of Orwell and because of a million other dead bodies and great men and great women in Spain eighty years prior we were here now.

In the stillness.

And as we left the closed-in streets of the village, we emerged out onto a plain. The wind cut across it. I looked over to you, and I knew you had been thinking the same things I had been thinking because there are many different men who go to war, but in the end, in the thick of it, they become one. And every man takes his poison and corrupts himself differently, but they are all trapped in that same place forever, trapped hating, trapped in singularity. Begging for the enemy to step forth. And I wondered if the fascists had thought similar thoughts on the ridgeline when a young Englishman lobbed a grenade into his bunker. But to grant humanity to the enemy in a time like this was a trivial matter, it could be swatted away as a lethargic mosquito. Or crushed, and though your own blood would bleed from the mosquito's body, you still felt the exuberance of a killed enemy.

We had poisoned ourselves before the Humvee ever rolled to a stop on the outskirts of the city.

"Here," the driver said in Kurdish. And six of us unloaded from the vehicle and made for the nearest building, our hearts pounding, our fingers begging. Jaws clenched. We walked carefully, mindful of mines we could not have seen. I should have thought of home or thought of a woman or thought of staying alive, but I only thought of Spain, of pine-needled floors of forests. I could smell no pines, only dirt kicking into my nostrils, coating my throat. And you knew if we did not walk with purpose we would be mistaken for the enemy and gunned down. So you led us to the first building, and you ushered the other four of our number inside and once they were situated you turned to me, and we left, headed on to the next house.

You could see its silhouette in the night. The half-completed second story was crowned with unfinished pillars reaching for the sky, rebar prodding to the night against the dull orange haze of fires lit on rooftops to our rear. There were cars strewn about the field between the building and us.

And you laughed. "What a good fucking way to get blown up," you said, "wandering through a junkyard on the front line at three in the morning."

In that moment, I did not feel sorry or afraid, only remorse at the thought that we both might have died before you ever got the chance to get that kill, that one you were sure of. That one that was so important for you that it became important for me. We were lucky, you and I, for that scrapyard held no mines that our feet found. And in the next house we made our way to the incomplete second story, spread blankets down, and lay under the dark sky. Jets scuttled through the air above us, letting their bombs cascade around our position like whimsical grains of salt. They did not care if we were the enemy or friendly. Even if they did miss their mark it was only another dead Kurd or Arab to them, not a white American. Who cares if a man dies from your mistakes on the other side of the world? So long as you do not have to observe the body or observe the wake or the mothers ripping coffins from the pallbearers, tearing the lids open, bellowing to their god, trying to crawl in the casket with their son. What did they matter?

And still I could only think of Spain. And I hoped I was living up to something worthwhile. And I could feel the hate in me. And I wished that the enemy would show itself, just for another chance to take him away.

You and I have both heard that to kill is a sin. And that a lust for ending life is shameful. But this too must be heard: The life of the enemy is no life at all, and that is how wars have been and are to be fought. Any redeeming qualities that their humanity may once have afforded them were burned up with the bodies of the journalists and the Yazidis. And who is god to hoard all the power of life for himself? That is what war is for, no? For men to play chess with soldiers as soldiers play god with the enemy. Through the barrel of that rifle, you deify yourself. God is a chromoly spiral.

"They'll come," you said in the morning. "I can feel it."

From across the flames of our little fire on the rooftop, I could see the scar on your neck clearly now. I could see the tendon tight beneath it. "I hope they do."

The winds that had cut across the plain the previous night now picked up. Gusts buffeted the walls of our building. Sand rose above the houses in the city. And somewhere in that city, a fire was lit from tires. We could smell them. Black smoke churned in the sky, and it wafted toward us.

Only a short time later that day, with the sun high but obscured by the sand and the smoke, you would see them in the scope of your rifle as I saw them in the scope of mine, and we would have our first real chance to fire a weapon on a man and know with any certainty that he would feel the bullet. So you must breathe calmly and let your finger rest on the trigger of a rifle as a god's must and see the shadowy figures in dark clothes scrambling through rubble. You must choose one for yourself, and I will take the other. It is only the enemy now—the fascists.

And you squeeze. The rifle recoils.

And you must hope that any redeeming qualities of their humanity are not enough to overcome the weight of their ideology. Not enough to overcome the burning men in cages. Not enough to overcome the rib-thin Jews lined up and shot. Not enough to overcome the Armenians marched through this very same desert and killed on the blood-red banks of the Euphrates. Not enough to overcome the torture or the pain or the wails of women or the bitter apathy of the rest of the world. Not enough to overcome the sunken ships. Not enough to overcome Guernica and Auschwitz and Graziani and Diyarbakir and Sinjar and Jakarta and Wounded Knee. Not enough to overcome the lynchings and the bombings and the nightmares visited upon other faces, other places that you may never have known and never have seen, but in that moment you wished you could know their suffering just to pour further justification into the recoil of the rifle.

Then you fire again.

11 December 2018: Qereçox, Rojava, Noktaya Şehîd Kendal Breizh:

Requalifying on the AK put me in the top five shooters of the Tabûr—good enough for an M-16 if they ever get delivered as promised (they won't). Likely, they will go the same as starting the Academy or all these promised operations or even the radios. This shit is fucking Jarhead. & we are all Swofford. We shoot into the hillsides. We study Kurdish we will never speak to a Kurd. & we hydrate. & we eat. I cooked today, at least that has improved in my time here. Everyone is losing their shit. I can't blame them. Military training seems pointless once you know that you are among the best-trained units in the YPG... & the least utilized. The average YPG infantryman receives two weeks of training before heading to the front. What the fuck are we still doing here in the rear? "You are not ready," they say. It is a toll on one's mind. We are all fragile now, to speak is like walking on eggshells. Agît snapped at me today just because I said I was waiting on him to finish room-clearing drills. My meals were good, & a bowl of şîşa was a nice way to unwind at the end of the day, though the conversations with Brûsk, Mavros, & Soro were a bit heavy—demoralizing even—under the haze of hookah smoke in our room. It seems hopeless. The Kurds don't know what we go through here—to be here, else they would not hold us back like this. & the rain never stops for long.

"If it didn't rain how else would the trash wash away?" – Soro, watching the river rise & flood over, trash flowing downstream.

* * *

I can feel myself inching toward some inevitable edge. *I was nearly there today when shooting in the deluge. "Fuck this, I'm gonna go home & work on fucking Harleys." & I would like that. I think it may snap within me sometime soon. Knowing the opportunity to go home is only 14 days away makes it all the harder to convince myself to stay, even if there are operations going. I must remember what I came here for. But I must also accept that life after Rojava will happen sooner or later, no matter how hard it may be to leave all this behind; no matter how hard it may be to stay.*

Warren Stoddard II

First Bloom of Spring

It is a bad time to be alone when the sun finally breaks through.

The people are laughing together and walking by, but you have never apologized. That was always you. You meant what you said, and you meant what you did, and you would do it and say it all again just so you felt *alive*.

What do you have?

There are people walking by. They are laughing. They are smiling. They are together, and the sun is on their faces after so long a winter and they are happy, and here you sit alone in the shade.

24 December 2018: Siwêdîk, Rojava:

Our big, final, crucible of a training session went off today. As we woke the rain was pouring down. "It ain't training if it ain't raining!" We loaded up all our gear–me carrying the Biksî with a 100-round belt, 300 rounds of 7.62x54 ammo in a backpack plus body armor, my AK with 150 rounds of ammunition for it & food & water to last three days & we headed out into the valley. We hopped a few stones to cross the river–its waters already rising. Some feet got wet–more on that later. After some time walking alongside the river in the rain, we set up camp in the woods on the bank & laid in the mud for an hour. By the time actual exercises in ambushing & reacting to contact began I was shivering & the knuckles of my fingers ached. Then came some sîzma–stealth. & by the time medical drills began we were all deliriously miserable with wet & cold–laughing hysterically at anything. "Alright, if we could get just a hint of seriousness here," Zafer said, wringing out his soaked beanie. Nothing makes such good comedy as absolute misery. We ate knockoff chicken spam from cans with our knives or combat spoons. The nan was drenched & falling apart in our hands by the time it made it to our mouths. & I was pissing myself, watching the urine run from the bottom of my pants both for the comic relief & to warm myself up for a bit. The rain had been pounding all morning & into the afternoon without abatement. Our final exercise was to be a recon of a notional enemy position on the other side of the hill across the river, which by this point was a torrent of downhill water risen five feet above its normal level. Really, we should have known better. Zafer briefed us as he & Haqî began to cross the river. On Haqî's first attempt he sank waist deep not 10 feet from the bank of the expanse. Zafer said he saw a better crossing point upstream; he would lead the way this time. "I'm going to show you how to cross tactically," he said with his goggles foggy & his prized M-16 held above his head. He waded out some 15 feet or so. The current was quick. "You'll hold your weapon over your hea-" he called back to us all from where we watched on the bank, becoming submerged in the frigid waters on the last syllable. As he went under, we erupted into laughter. When he surfaced again, I knew by the look on his face that it wasn't funny anymore. I dropped the Biksî & undid my backpack as he began to gurgle calls for help, & as I hit the water I threw my body armor back towards the shore & made for Zafer as quick as I could. He was in full panic mode by the time I reached him. "You're alright, man," I said & smiled, leading him to a tree to grab hold of, "I thought you were going to die, you fucking idiot." Hevals daisy chained together & reached out a shovel to pull us to safety. As soon as we hit dry land Zafer turned to me & said he was going back for the M-16. He had dropped it in his panic to get above water. "Well, fuck it. I'm already wet, so why not?" There was no way we were going to find the thing, but we tried for a good 5 minutes before giving it up. My vision was blurry & my bitching was slurred from the cold. I stripped down & took a space blanket from my pack & wrapped my bare torso with it. Zafer did the same. Friends gathered about & took up our gear on their shoulders & helped us navigate the way back to the nokta with candy & lucid conversation. & the space blanket worked—don't say watching Bear Grylls on

MBC Action can't teach you anything. The river was churning turbid brown water at the ford we had crossed earlier in the day. We checked up & down stream—nothing. Only one option: link arms & walk across in fours so that we might make a mass large enough to avoid being swept downstream. I wish someone had a picture of that moment. Two naked idiots in space blankets wading the river, helped along by people all stupid enough to play in the rain on Christmas Eve. We gathered every heater in the tabûr in the common room, warmed up together & took naps until the şawarma delivery came for supper. Then movies & bullshitting until bed. I'm glad Zaf is alright. He wants to go looking for his rifle tomorrow with water flooding his already burst eardrum. I won't dive in, but I'll tag along for the comedy factor. With this cycle of training complete, we've got a week off now, hopefully within which we finally find out who is going on operations. Maybe they'll really happen as well. At the very least it is long enough of a time off to start getting pissed about doing nothing to want to go through bullshit like today all over again.

25 December 2018: Qereçox, Rojava, Noktaya Şehîd Kendal Breizh:

Merry fucking Christmas & happy 6 months in Syria to me. To celebrate, all of us cleaned all the weapons & lounged in the common room watching movies. Not the Christmas sort, but oh well if everyone else is a Grinch. After lunch we held tabûr photo day, & then I went with Aşîtî, Breizh, & Zafer to recover his M-16 from the riverbed. The truck got stuck in the mud of the riverbank on the way out & took some pushing to get it free again. We parked it on the side of a mountain across the valley & hiked back to where "the incident" took place. Zaf & I waded into the water & he poked around with a stick for all of about ten seconds before he was lifting his rifle over his head again. All's well that ends well. Sheep for supper & a hookah/ whiskey session to cap the day off. We had a bottle of fine stuff we managed to get ahold of—"Red Daniel" they call it. 6 months. I never thought I'd make it & now that it's here I'm not even headed home. There must be some screws loose in me somewhere & a couple of bolts down tight. I love these guys. How do you leave? How do you cast this entire life you've made here aside? Kill it all for good? I don't know, & I am terrified to find out. But for now, I am happy & in good spirits & a little drunk. "Operations after Christmas" means tomorrow. Let's get to Hajin.

Warren Stoddard II

Marienplatz

I am sitting at an outdoor table at the wursthaus. My table is red-checkered and marked by streaks from wiping. Where the table wiper's streaks do not go there are crumbs on the checkers from whoever ate here last, but I am in the shade and the beer is cold and served in tall glasses whose branding matches that of its coaster. It is a crisp, dark beer, and I take a sip and wipe some froth from my mustache. What a thing it would be to die here in the shade in the afternoon.

Before me, people stream through a burgundy brick archway in bunches. They are carrying shopping bags and purses and boxes of newly bought shoes. They are talking on the phone or they are texting their friends. A few of them are watching where they walk.

There are many others seated at these red-checkered tables. Midafternoon is a busy time of day to get a beer. It is lubricating their conversations. A woman to my left can be heard talking on the phone over the chiming of church bells in the distance.

"You know, I think after Munich I want to go to some small town and get some real *culture.* It just seems so hard to find real German life here in the big city. Everything seems so *Americanized.*" She is sipping red wine in a biergarten, and I know that as soon as she leaves the friendly confines of her

Airbnb she will be shouting to the middle-aged manager of a small inn, who speaks no English, about the unavailability of free Wi-Fi. She will scream loudly at the woman as though raising her volume will improve the odds that the manager will understand her. "Germany sucks," she will declare to her family when she returns from her backpacking trip four days before Christmas, "for the most part, but I really liked Munich." Now she hangs up the phone, scrolls through her device for a bit, downs the last of her wine as if it were cheap vodka, and walks away leaving seven Euros too many on the red checkered table.

The waitress comes and pockets the money, wipes the table down, turns to me and sees my empty beer glass. She nods her head toward it. I nod mine in return. And soon she is back. She takes my empty glass and sets a full one down on the coaster. She leaves, and I sip and enjoy the sound of the leaves rustling together mixing with the hubbub of conversation spoken in many languages.

A new person has come to that same table to my left. This one is a nervous looking man of about thirty-five. He is wearing a gray business suit and is carrying a briefcase that seems as though it holds nothing. The briefcase only exists in his hand as a way to confirm to himself that he is a businessman. He is scribbling something with a pencil on a yellow legal pad like one who fears death.

Men who fear death should never write in pen. The finality of it, the totality and forced recognition of one's errors is more akin to dying than most anything else a man can do in his life.

The man frantically rubs his eraser across something he has just written. The waitress comes to ask him if he will order anything. He does not, and the waitress asks him to leave.

Again, the waitress and I exchange nods over my empty beer glass, and she brings a full one to replace it. I see that my coaster has a definitive ring of sweat imprinted on it as I lift the glass to my lips to take a sip, with the hum of the leaves and the conversation in many languages in my ear.

Further down the row of tables there is a large family speaking in a language I cannot understand. They are six in total—two women, two men, and two young boys who both stare into an iPhone they each hold with one hand. It is evident they are playing some sort of game—something nostalgic that makes them yearn for a bygone era. Romans with gladiuses and the choking stench of slavery. Knights in shining armor and the slow death brought on by famine. Grenadiers in Napoleon's ranks with knees buckling and feet giving out from frostbite in the Russian winter. If these two boys had been born but a century earlier in some Austrian village, they would soon be shuffled to the front to die screaming in an artillery barrage in the trenches. One of the boys throws back his head in frustration. Evidently, he has lost. The women are engrossed in conversation while the men look on at the boys. How will they teach them to die?

It is a hard lesson to learn and to teach, for men have spent centuries dying as young boys in foreign mud in foreign lands. And so it is a deeply ingrained fear—death. Yet it must be taught. But to begin to learn this, death must first be understood as something more than a game. It is not a plaything. Dying is not to be toyed with. It is the end. But to look death in the face and ride to meet its reality is far preferred to be running from it screaming and crying to hide someplace where it will still catch you anyway. Thus, death must become a circus to men not brave enough to come to grips with it—for those afraid to end a sentence, a story, a nostalgic remembrance.

The family rises and pays the bill and walks away. The waitress comes and clears their table and my beer is replaced with a full one. I sip it and enjoy the sound of the leaves rustling and the conversation in many languages. I notice the man in the gray suit sitting on the ground with his back against the burgundy-bricked arch now, still frantically scribbling on the yellow legal pad.

The waitress glances in his direction as she leads two new people to the table to my left. The first is a man of twenty-seven, and the second is a beautiful woman. Her blonde hair shines even in the dying light of an approaching dusk.

The pair sit and chat together. It is evident that he does not know that she is in love with someone else. She wears pearl earrings and has a Louis Vuitton set beside her feet. The rings on their fingers look new. And he is wearing a five-thousand-dollar suit. They appear to be on their honeymoon. They quickly finish a bottle of champagne as I finish another beer. Then something peculiar happens. She orders a hefeweizen, he a Moscato. And they both sip and then turn distractedly away as if they are bored.

By now, I am drunk and thinking of the war.

The man scribbling on the yellow legal pad has finished what he has been writing and is walking this way.

The waitress nods toward my near-empty glass, but I wave my hand to signal I am finished. I ask for the check.

The woman at the table to my left sits with crossed legs, and her beer and her golden hair both take on an amber light with the impending sundown. The man she is with has bought her. She is with him for money, and he is a fool to believe that this will be a thing that lasts. He will go from her to another beautiful young woman who he will outfit in pearl earrings and a Louis Vuitton. Rich men always believe they can buy love and bravery.

The man in gray hands a yellow piece of paper to the waitress as I am paying my bill. She looks tired, as if she will grant him the favor of reading this thing only one time—that it will be the final time unless it brings about some earth-shaking revelation. The man's eyes are burning with resolve and desperation. His pencil is yellow in his coat pocket.

I am looking at the beautiful woman with the bored expression and the blonde hair. I stand from my seat. In the time between now and when I speak to her, I will find some words to say. I will pray to god that she speaks English, and I will scribble frantically in my mind to find the words that will lift her from her seat, have her down her beer, and leave her purse and take my outstretched hand. We will walk a while. I know a place not far from here. It is near the river and shaded and very old. Headstones line the dirt pathways and the sun cuts through the little gaps in the leaves, casting dappled swathes of dancing light on the ground between the dead. It is a quiet place where you do not feel alone and the world does indeed still turn at the end of it all, and that is ok.

Together, the woman on my arm and I will be walking slowly, reading some of the headstones as we pass, wondering what it all means. And then we will see the man in gray and the waitress walking towards us along the path, holding each other close, talking in hushed tones. As we pass them, we will nod politely, and they in return. And I will see the pencil sticking up from the man's coat pocket, the eraser worn down to where it would be of no use.

31 December 2018: Qereçox, Rojava, Noktaya Şehîd Kendal Breizh:

"I sure hope you don't die mate. That'd be real depressing" - Berxwedan, early morning, drinking coffee.

& so it would. But sooner or later you figure out it was all just happening in your own head anyway. Nothing changes. Maybe just a descent into a further figment of your own imag-ination. I suppose this isn't funny to anyone but us, but what's the point in fearing death? It comes for us all eventually & life will go on with or without that one ending being. My life lives inside me. That can never be taken. It is not that I believe I am going to die—I certainly will do my best to avoid that at all costs. & it is not that I am unafraid. But these things must be reckoned with at some point in one's life. I think I have been reckoning with them for a long time. When I get out of this, I want to find a quiet piece of the world for myself where my mind & paranoia are not being constantly bombarded, though I do not know if I have it in me to sit quietly back & watch the world unfold. After this operation I think I am done with this place, barring some vast change of heart or circumstances (both of which are known to happen emphatically & at random). Yet 6 months is a long time to fry your brain as I have here; how long may it take to uncook myself? I long to go home & spend time with Noelle where we do nothing but sit in comfortable silence. Anything. I don't care what it is. But first things first. Aşîtî & I picked up the Dragunovs from the Academy. The rest of the day until well after nightfall was spent qualifying & zeroing all manner of scopes to their likely rifles. I had my pick of the SVD or M-16. I chose the latter—less weight to lug around.

The rifle I'll carry is the one so many toy guns in my youth were modeled after. It feels like holding home in my hands. It belongs with me. Like I've been training with it my whole life. The weather is still wet & cold & muddy & miserable. Our winter vacation to the tropical south Syrian paradise of Hajin will be a welcome reprieve. Sunny skies & balmy temperatures are in the forecast all week. But there is no forecast for what else we will find there. We know little aside from the fact that we will be working in sniper teams. I don't even know who my spotter will be. It'll all reveal itself in time. I've come to accept lack of information as a part of daily life here; there is no way around it, no YPG handbook to consult. Only take it 1 day at a time. The next 14 will be at the front. Happy New Year.

Warren Stoddard II

To Those I Have Killed

I suppose I am not sorry for what I have done. I only wish that I didn't have to. I wish that you had lived a better life. I wish you had thought more clearly. Then again maybe it is best you did not, then I may be where you are now and you writing this letter thinking of the rounds you fired and the hate you felt and the pain you inflicted on mothers, sisters, and brothers-in-arms.

The pain is another thing. I feel none of it over you. I watched you die. I watched the panicked frantic scrambling of your comrades around the hood of the car towards the passenger door to try and save you. And I fired again. I would fire again if I could, but your friends came to their senses and drove away in a cloud of dust that quickly dissipated on the wind under a clear sky.

There were so many rounds being thrown at you that you must have felt invincible. We all do. When you hear the heat singing off the metal above your head or the tearing whoosh of mortars incoming and the pricks of bullets against stone it is hard to believe that one of them could catch you. But one does. And I know it was me. That maelstrom of lead was all ringing out for you from our rooftop, and why not? No one was returning fire toward us. There was only you in that little blue van with other black-clad friends of yours—enemies of ours. Everyone in front of us was the enemy, they said. Everyone. Especially you.

I know it was me. Those other occupants in the blue van with you were all so calm. It was as though those around me were firing towards the placidity of an oil painting. But I had a scope. And I adjusted for the range. And the windage. And I watched as hundreds or thousands of rounds were fired toward you from my rooftop—all falling short of you. Landing in the dirt, maybe ricocheting up the berm towards you in that little blue van, but you just sat there and watched us.

I know what you were thinking.

Because I have thought it too.

"They will not touch me. Surely."

And you go about your business. Through my scope I saw someone leave the driver's side of the car, crouching down behind the van. Adjusting something, lifting something, doing *something* behind cover. That cover was you. You in your impenetrable glass castle. You beyond the range of the AK-47, all those rounds.

But I had a scope.

Through that scope I saw worlds burning and matter colliding. I saw bodies in the sun. I saw hatred and overzealous propaganda, your black flag and your uncut beard. I saw the rubble behind that little blue van, and I saw your friend crouching over there. I saw your nonchalance. I saw what you had done, I saw the sun reflecting off the untinted front-passenger-side window, and through the corner of my eye I saw brass refuse spilling from the rifles of my friends.

But most importantly I saw you.

And I fired.

And at once I saw panic in that car. I saw scrambling pandemonium as the bullet hit glass and then you. Blood surely spattered across the fabric ceiling of the van. The driver swung his door open and ducked behind the hood of the vehicle. And now I was firing again and again, each round finding its home in the side of that faded blue van, people in the back ducking, the driver running around the side to your door before he thought better of it as another round found what it was aimed towards. It was you.

And then the driver jammed the car down into gear and sped off with you and a terrified few others. But you were not afraid anymore. You never were. I suppose you can thank me for that. Maybe I should have warned you first, but then again, I did not warn any of the others, and none of you afforded a warning to me.

If it makes you feel better, I never talk about it, and I don't suppose I ever will.

Killing is not easy, and it feels like illness inside of me, and sometimes I wake in the night thinking of it, and I am still there when I close my eyes, wishing perhaps that you did not have to die. But I suppose I am not sorry for all the things I have done.

1 January 2019: Qereçox, Rojava, Noktaya Şehîd Kendal Breizh:

Gary King once said to me at his table, hands stained black from oil & grease, pictures of panheads & the Ia Drang Valley in '69 tacked to his wall: "You're gonna get there & have a moment where you say to yourself, 'This is so fucked up!'" 8 hours to Hajin. Let's go.

1 January 2019: Raqqa Governorate Countryside, Syria:

It took us over an hour at least just to get through the maze of market squares, side streets, & regime checkpoints in the city of Qamişlo. The hilarity of it was not lost on us. We ate nuts for lunch from a bag passed around & gorged upon. Then, we played "pass the foreigner" once we got to Shaddadi. The commander we were told to ask for was nowhere to be found. Instead, we were made to wait at "the academy:" A horror story that seems to keep repeating itself.

"Smart money's on 3 cups of çay before we find this guy."
– Haqî, waiting at a command post in Shaddadi.

But they fed us a good meal of roasted chicken & tomatoes & oranges & rice & after a bit we were on our way again. At a pit-stop for gas I managed to run over—no, to bulldoze—over the top of 3 of the 6 trees in sight. The bed of the truck wedged itself on top of one of them & we needed the help of several dismayed Arabs to get the Hilux moving again, we left them mourning over the flattened saplings, & then the transmission almost blew trying to follow this guy at blistering speeds along dirt roads. But eventually we wound up at an abandoned school near Raqqa. Sason—the man we'd been sent to find—read the small piece of paper we handed him & told us our mission: we'd be split up into 2 three-man teams at the front—now in the south of Hajin—covering the advancing lines from elevated positions. A group effort on supper (Haqî cooked & we felt bad about it). & then the diesel fumes of heaters clouded the room we slept in. To the cebhe in the morning.

Warren Stoddard II

Through All That Angry Air:

The language of the war against ISIS

The silence of the room is broken only by the chirp of a radio and the concussive booms of mortars on the other side of the wall. Dust falls from the rafters. I am lying on a mattress on the floor. A young Arab fighter hands me a cigarette, an AK-47 across his lap. And I tell another with my eyes that I am done fighting as I press a bandage tight to my leg. Blood–hot–runs through my fingers.

"They come for you," he says in Kurdish.

Some time ago, a few years or more, in an undergraduate class about the history of the English language, the question was put to me how war–how it being such a different way of living and dying–shapes and mutates the ways we communicate. Being as yet inexperienced in the matter, the answer I gave was something along the lines of "I don't know." Language is hardly capable of describing it.

Following my graduation from Texas State University in May of 2018, I joined the Kurdish YPG, a militia in the northeast of Syria (an area also known in Kurdish as Rojava). I flew into Iraqi Kurdistan and stayed at a safe house for some days with some other western volunteers. I'd climbed mountains in Iceland, and drank beer in Munich, rode a Harley through the west Texas desert and rebuilt the motor in a motel room, but I'd never been human trafficked before. We were smuggled like rebranded cattle across the Iraqi-Syrian border in the dead of night and ushered to a place called The Academy.

I expected to be launched straight into the fight against the Islamic State. Instead, many months of ideological training ensued—the Kurds practice an ideology of feminism, ecology, and a decentralized socialist form of democracy all contained under the umbrella of Democratic Confederalism. There were cultural snags and mishaps, friends died in far off battles that we were told we would be shielded from—no more of us would fight—die, and there were widespread propaganda campaigns headlined by us westerners. We begged to go to the front. And we were told to make more propaganda. And we begged all the more to carry our rifles and grenades down to the Hajin Pocket and help in the fight against the last vestiges of Daesh (a word of Arabic slang for ISIS meaning invader, it carries as much heat and anger behind it as calling a Black person the "N" word would. And Daesh is just as offended).

Our unit was made up of mostly English speakers, and our integration into the local Kurdish society was minimal. So

English was all we spoke along with some mutilated form of Kurmanji. At best we could muster something like Eng-manji —Kurdish mostly, with English words and wild cheradiphic gesticulations to fill the gaps in our fluency. That language of the world that is mostly universal wherever one goes.

As our language skills progressed it became apparent how little of a spoken or written language is needed to survive and get by. Kurmanji, thanks to generations of ethnic cleansing, is still not officially a written language, with multitudes of dialects and ways of spelling simple words. For example, the Kurdish word for fire can be spelled agir, egir, agîr, êgir, axir, ahîr and so on to infinity. Language is a very simple thing that we educated types have done our best to turn into a labyrinth of pitfalls and exceptions waiting around every corner to snare the unsuspecting speaker. As a result, it is best maintained orally. Such is the reason why so many of those songs of the ancients have survived—the oral tradition is far more important than the written one. As a writer it pains me to say that, but it makes it no less true.

This forbidden language of Kurmanji was outlawed by the Byzantine empire, the Ottomans, the Safavids; Salahadîn (a born Kurd) even shunned the language of his birth in favor of the Prophet's Arabic; the modern states of Turkey, Iran, Iraq, and Syria have all at one point or another in their history banned the speaking and teaching of Kurdish in an effort to eradicate Kurdish culture and tradition. Yet still it presses on. It was spoken in dark alleyways and behind locked doors. And it became a language of resistance, cemented by centuries of struggle and conflict into the memories of proud Kurds throughout the region.

War binds experiences to your soul. It is what saved the Kurdish language.

After many months of begging and pleading with the command, we were given the opportunity to go to the front line. By this point, the city of Hajin—the last capital, and the largest city held by the so called "Caliphate"—had mostly fallen. The bulk of the fighting was taking place south of Hajin proper. The front line was just outside the city of Ash Sha'fah. We were told we would now be heading there. "You will go as snipers. Stay somewhere in the back, stay safe, gain some experience in how the front-line works. Come home safe. No injuries, no şehîds (martyrs). You will not be in the fighting." A refrain we had heard many times over the months.

But hear this: FUCK. THAT. SHIT.

We met with cebhe (frontline) commanders and immediately began weaseling our way forward. "Is this close enough?" Of course not. "How close do you want to be?" Piştî cebhe—we were itching for the fight, *the very front line*, and then we were there. Due to five years' worth of western volunteers smuggling gear into Syria, we boasted far superior arms and equipment than the Arab QSD who were doing the bulk of the fighting. They loved us for our night vision, my M-16, our ability to quickly zero a Dragunov scope to the rifle. We made many friends among the Arabs, found our way to the very front unit, and once there we kept pushing forward hundreds of meters at a time, moving in a lightning-quick advance by cover of night down the banks of the Euphrates. We joked one night after advancing some two and a half kilometers that this must be what the Mongols felt like when they were amassing their empire. ISIS must have given up and fled to Turkey. There were none of them left, and this advance was simply to look good on the news reels.

There was little resistance in the suburbs—pot shot exchanges—little more than a few cursory rounds across the rubble of no-man's land to let the other side know we were there. There were some mortar bombardments and artillery barrages that thudded into the earth and spaced out the time spent waiting during the day.

And there were the air strikes; they were beautiful from far off, hitting every small light made in the distance in the dead of night, killing those who would kill you. You saw them first, a burst of sparks and dust a mile or so off, and then a concussion wave hit the building and jostled the bricks in their mortar, before finally you heard the roar of the jet and the boom of the missile hitting long after first seeing the sparks. But they were more terrifying and amazing from close. If you heard the report of the missile impacting at the same time that it hit the ground, there was a good chance it would be the last sense you ever felt. I woke one night to a jet diving low, sending a missile screeching overhead—a flash of white light roaring and ripping apart the sky. It hit not 20 meters off. My world shook enough to fall apart. Shrapnel, and debris, whole bricks and bits of rebar rained down on the rooftop where we slept. I covered myself with the blanket as a child might. Nothing can get you there. Under the blanket you are safe. I rolled to the wall and ducked my head under my body armor once I realized what was happening. After the rain of rocks and metal ceased, a stream of English, Arabic, and Kurdish curse words flowed from our end of the radio towards whoever had called in the strike. I did not sleep again so long as jets were flying above us. Their reports sounded in the near distance throughout the night, clearing a path for our advance south.

In the morning, with dawn's soft light creeping in on the peripherals of the world, we lit fires from found wood on the roofs of houses to keep warm, making tea, trying to make ourselves understood to the Arabs and Kurds we were fighting alongside. We were now in the city of Ash Sha'fah.

The wind was blowing harder than the days previous. It kept our bones chilled even as the sun emerged (Syria is a cold fucking place in the wintertime; don't let anyone tell you different). With the wind in their favor, Daesh lit a tire fire somewhere near the city center. Its black smoke billowed toward us, and the air strikes all but stopped. There were no targets to see. Then, of course, came a fortuitous sandstorm. You could hardly see 75 meters at times. ISIS, using their most favored tactic, began to advance with the windswept sand. Mortars, both ours and theirs, incoming and outgoing, were hitting all around our little house on the front line. The team nearest us was pinned down by a Daesh sniper. Then came a DShK (a very large Russian machine gun usually mounted to the bed of a pickup truck or the roof of a tank). It was firing our direction. When its bullets found the wall outside, dust would rain from the rafters.

A call came over the radio. Our friends in the next house over had somehow gotten pinned on the roof of their building. All the English speakers in my sniper team had gone to the rear to get the water we'd been without for 24 hours. Some gesturing and broken Kurmanji followed. Only one of the QSD fighters I was with spoke Kurdish. The rest were Arabs. From this conversation I gathered that we had to go to the roof, find the sniper, and give our comrades some cover. So we did. One man with an angry countenance and a black hat pulled low over his face grabbed a PKM machine gun, I was second in line, carrying my M-16 with the scope, and a kid no older than 18 behind me hefted a Kalashnikov onto that rooftop.

They say that time slows when you are in a firefight. I am not sure that is the case. It is rather that the firefight unfolds so slowly in reality as opposed to what we see in cinema and what our mind regulates backwards for us to understand. There is no way you could be so calm as bullets and shells are humming through the air at thousands of feet per second. But you are. Battle is as serene and peaceful a place as any. At the time of the fighting I was no more stressed than I would have been in rush hour traffic. You fire, and you look again, and you fire. You feel shockwaves in the earth beneath you. And you think you may have hit something, but there is never any way to tell.

The machine gunner set up to my left, the AK-47 wielding kid to my right. I looked through my scope to the rubble of a building. Two black-clad figures ran through my field of view, and I fired once for each of them. I hope to whatever god there is—theirs or yours or to the Flying Spaghetti Monster—that I killed them. I hope that more than anything I have ever hoped, and that is the best I can do to describe it.

Then the wall exploded by my face.

And I was running back to the stairwell. The two I had come to the roof with were nowhere in sight. Typical QSD. I found them on the stairs, and they asked if I was alright. My heart was pounding euphorically, and I knew in that instant how it was that men became addicted to combat.

I felt some sort of pain—the kind you feel when someone throws a rock at you and hits you right on the bone. Not hard. Just a deadened feeling in the limb. I thought I was fine. Maybe a mortar hit close by and sent some rocks into my leg and foot and armpit. I kept patting at myself, finding nothing until I felt blood on my hands—warm and wet. Sticky, slimy somehow all the same.

A curse-ridden rendition of the Happy Birthday song popped into my head.

"*How fucked are you now? You're surely fucked now.*"

"I'm hit;" that was all I could manage over the radio. The sniper we were after got me. Or maybe it was the high-powered Russian machine gun. Or maybe it was a grenade. Maybe a mortar round exploded on that rooftop. What it was that bit me matters little, but the fact that the bullet punched through a wall and was probably misdirected by a few inches of concrete saved my head from turning to paste like so many dropped watermelons.

And so here I am now—these Arabs have never even seen a tourniquet. I put one on myself and bandage the wound in my thigh. There is blood pooling in my boot as well, and under my right arm, but those wounds seem minor in comparison. I ask the Arab kid for a cigarette and stress smoke it in about two drags and am soon out the door on the machinegunner's shoulders screaming at him to “Go!” in Kurdish he does not understand and he mutters something in Arabic as mortars hit all around us and shrapnel whistles through the air and in my head in English I am in awe of the parade of auditory sensations running through my ears and mind, wondering if I will die, soaking in life’s beauty in the thick of a heavy mortar bombardment on the banks of the Euphrates.

He sprinted some hundred meters through all that angry air to get me to safety. We did not even know one another’s names.

And then a long journey comes back to the rear to where I will sit surrounded by people speaking some sick Arabic-Kurdish lovechild of a language that I can little make sense of or make myself comprehended in beyond charades. But we understand each other.

That is what war does to language. I can tell you all about what it is that happened, but that does not adequately describe what it is like to be engaged in combat with an enemy. Language fails war the same way it fails love. Combat was both the best, the most wonderful, joyous experience of my life and the absolute worst, full of terror and hatred and pain indescribable. Silence and deafening noise.

There was an *Esquire* article written by William Broyles Jr. in the 1980's about Vietnam titled "Why Men Love War." In it Broyles says, "I suffered, I was there. You were not. Only those facts matter. Everything else is beyond words to tell." You will likely never experience combat, you will never fall in loathing love with it, and I hope that you don't, but the experience is the only adequate way of describing the thing.

Language is of little importance in the matter anyhow.

3 January 2019: Hajin, Syria:

We woke 11 km north of Hajin proper. On the dirt road in front of the headquarters where we'd slept people were coming & going, their arms laden with goods, with goats trailing behind them, going about their daily lives as the black smoke of explosions rose from the city behind them. After lunch we loaded up & headed out, driving to the musical accompaniment of Taylor Swift, Ke$ha, & gangster rap. Mine & Haqî's radio call signs reflected this—he is Swifty, I'm Ke$ha. The ruins of Hajin city looked every bit as Berlin might have in 1945 & then some. Nearly every building was a blasted-out shell of framework. The road zigzagged left & right to avoid 15-foot deep airstrike craters. The scene was utterly devoid of the living. Dead Daesh outnumbered the wild dogs. The Americans seemed to airstrike strategically, however. Their command post was the nicest building for miles around—not a chip had been pocked out of the three-story marble façade. The drone of their jets, low & lethal, levitated in our ears. That noise is sure to become a constant companion in the coming days. After waiting around for a while for the higher-ups to hash it out, we headed to the second line.

"We're not the tip of the spear, but we're definitely getting the shaft!"—Haqî, after being told we may stay on the second line.

Or not. When we were asked if the second line was a good spot for us by our QSD guide, the answer was no. We wanted to be closer. "The front line?" Of course. Ask & you shall receive the closer you get to the action, apparently.

We were positioned at the very front 2 houses with mortars screeching above us, destined for some enemy position on the other side of the marsh that divided our position from the next suburb. In those suburbs & villages beyond the marsh–ISIS. We possessed far superior equipment than the QSD we were attached to; our night vision was the envy of everyone. They kept pointing to things, having us train our scopes on rustles in the bushes & whispers in the night. Only the scope we'd been given by the SDF commanders the night before didn't work, or we were too stupid to sort out how to use it. We stowed it in a bag in the truck–useless. Not that it was too sorely missed–any small light in the distance was immediately the target of a growing, diving roar & then buried by an airstrike. Sparks shattering in the distance. A delayed boom & the concussive wave that rattled the bricks in their mortar. Then a barrage of them. The earth shook. Two groups advanced to the nearest little village; heavy firefights broke out & they were forced to fall back. Then word came that we would be advancing too. Alan's team came across to our building & the six of us moved out with Emerîkî's tabûr. Down below, through the front doors of the building, a bridge stretched from our position to the other side of the marsh, like a thin infinity in the growing dark. On our side, bathed in warm light from one of the few streetlamps left, Aşîtî & Alan played rock, paper, scissors to decide which of the 2 of our sniper groups would advance first. Alan won, lucky sons of bitches. So we waited while they crossed. We waited, staring into the dark across the marsh where we knew the next group of buildings to be. Once they were in the village & the Humvees came back for us, gunshots split the night on fully automatic, their muzzle flashes bright & lingering as 4th of July sparklers.

"It's in God's hands now my son." - Berxwedan, waiting to load up on a Humvee, heavy sarcasm, as per usual.

We climbed on the roof of the Humvee, Aşîtî in front guiding the way with NVGs, me & Berx in back, talking shit. & as it rolled off, I began to slip, & with every jostle & lurch in the road, my grip loosened more & more. I felt my heart contract, pumping adrenaline. This is where I fucking die. Here. This is how. But just as my last foothold went, Berxwedan grabbed me & held me secure. I owe him one. Once in the village, we waited in pitch darkness, the shadows of the trees impenetrable, fingers on triggers—the Arabs & us all dead silent. It would either be ISIS or our friends coming to greet us. In the end, it was our friends. We helped them to clear the two buildings we would be occupying, finding no enemy soldiers, but plenty of loot—ghanima —coins & the like, & then we settled in for a cold night on the rooftops with airstrikes booming in the distance in Ash Sha'fah.

4 January 2019: Hajin, Syria:

Fires of desperation in the morning. Anything burns if you're cold enough. Airstrikes & mortars were hitting very close all day. The units behind us are firing at something, but we can see no targets out in no-man's land. It didn't take long for boredom to set in. Arabs like to shoot... at anything... birds, rocks, cats, whatever they saw. I helped a kid zero his Dragunov scope. Then a van was seen off in the hazy distance—blue—stopped on the ridge line. Filling up the gas tank? Spying on us? Laying IEDs? Who knows? Who cares? The whole tabûr opened up on the thing. AKs, Dragunovs, my M-16, the Biksî. Anything that could shoot was shot. The car was a ways off—maybe 500, 800 meters. I do not know if anyone else hit anything, but as I fired, I swore I could feel my bullets puncturing glass, flesh. & the car got out of there quick after my shots & the front was quiet again. Daesh drones overhead then, trying to drop grenades on our position. We shot them down with 12-gauge shotguns—a duck hunt. Near sundown I made my way across the courtyard to the other nokta & smoked hookah with the Arabs on the roof, mortars hitting not far off. Another fireworks show once darkness set in. The airstrikes & artillery were hitting 50 meters away at their closest, maybe closer. I can hear the shrapnel pinging off the brick walls of our room & clattering across the roof; just cover up with the blankets & try to get some sleep.

Warren Stoddard II

As All Wars Do

They were standing over me. Their faces were covered by masks. Their hats were camouflage and branded with the logos of college football teams. I could hear the jets circling overhead. The tourniquet bit into my leg.

"You're a long way from home now, aren't you son?"

"You'd think this far away I'd wind up with somebody besides an Aggie and a Sooner fixing me up."

They both laughed. "Sometimes you get what you get," the woman said.

Sometimes you do. American Marines were scrambling to and fro on the other side of the open doorway. Their mortars sounded like bank drive-through tubes as they were launched toward their destination. The sky was gray. I was bleeding.

Another instant before or after and it would have killed me—another inch left or right. "You're lucky," one of the two standing over me said. I nodded and felt hands grasp my thigh and with the unwinding of the tourniquet I felt a sweet orgasmic release run from my shin to my hip. They flipped me over. Pulling off my boot felt like razors running along my foot, sharp edge in, slicing to the bone. I bit the sleeve of my uniform. I felt pressure growing again in my thigh, then my foot. Bandages winding. They rolled me again onto my back and opened my uniform. They tacked another bandage under my arm, another two smaller ones—the kind you would find on the scraped knees of children—taped to my face. They handed me a pack of M&Ms.

"I haven't seen any of these in a while," I said.

They gave my bandages a once-over and helped me to sit. "You're very lucky," she said again, her eyes roaming across my body. The mortars were chucking.

"I'm just glad you're speaking English," I said.

"I'm sure you are." She was filling out a chart while I was tossing M&Ms into my mouth. Her eyes darted across my YPG patches and scarf to my injuries. "I think you're gonna be just fine," she said. "After this, I don't have any problem with you going back to kill more ISIS bad guys."

I cringed at her word choice, but my head perked up. "I'm going back tonight?" I asked. It was growing dark.

She looked at my foot, at my thigh—the pants of my uniform only drawn up around one leg. "No. You'll be laid up for a while. Tonight, you'll go to the hospital—Green Village. Hand them this and they'll take care of you. They'll clean you up. Proper."

The thought that I would not be returning to the front line hadn't yet crossed my mind. And why would it have? I'd left my rifle there like I would be coming back for it later. I could hear the chucking of the mortars. The jets were circling above. They were still fighting. They were fighting and dying and fighting and dying and I was eating M&Ms; the shells were hard—they crunched as I bit into them—the chocolate center soft and familiar. My friends were fighting and dying. But I would not. But I could walk. I could still fight; I was sure I could. I had not traveled here around the world merely to be slightly wounded and leave the war for others to win. I could fight. I stood from the stretcher as the nurses beckoned me towards the open doorframe and I immediately sank. My foot felt as though a 300-pound man was standing on it in cleats. Another step sent shockwaves of pain radiating from my thigh. "I'm not going back?" I asked.

"No," the man said. "Follow him." The Sooner handed me my boot and the chart and pointed toward a young middle eastern man in black camouflage, Syrian Democratic Forces patches on his arms that matched my own.

I hobbled toward him over hard-packed brown dirt. We made our way across the walled-in yard of the building. There were US military vehicles all around, painted that beige color. The jets were circling above. I leaned on the man. "Kurmanji dizanî?" I asked.

He knew no Kurdish. "Arabî mafîk?" he said.

I knew no Arabic.

He helped me into the back of the ambulance. Another Arab was sitting there, and he helped me into the stretcher. "Merheba," he said.

I parroted him in reply. He too spoke no Kurdish, only Arabic. So I sat in silence as the ambulance pulled away from the American medic station. Its wheels rolled over shards of shattered brick. The road was lined with craters punched into the earth by airstrikes. Its course thus wound about the holes in the ground–a dirt path smoothed out by bulldozers. The walls of the buildings we passed were in shambles. Rebar prodded at the clouds. I could still hear the jets circling.

From the stretcher I could see pine trees in the window that marked the northern edge of Hajin city. Their needles were covered in dust raised from the surface of the road by the coming and going of modern war. Vehicles laden with men, munitions, and food all trundled along this dusty road and powdered the branches, the bloodied men and women in the ambulances all watching the dust upon the trees through the windows, bidding a farewell to arms through dimming eyes, their lids heavy with morphine.

As all wars do, the trumpets and fanfare of revolution and religion had obliterated all other meaning to life here. The war had ripped this oldest civilization in the world to shreds. Kurds, Yazidis, Syriacs, Arabs, Christians, Jews, and Muslims had been scorched from their homes, starved out, decapitated, left in the sun to rot and have dogs tear at their corpses. It was all nothing but a passing joke to people in the west. "ISIS is everywhere." "ISIS bad guys." "Space ISIS." Hundreds of thousands of dead bodies lay in the ground or rotting in the sun and if I was lucky I had added to that count. If I was lucky I was now responsible for the instantaneous end of several human lives—all of whom believed themselves to be the most important such lives on the earth—all of whom believed themselves to be on the side of the good—all of whom knew alone how much their lives meant to them—how much they wanted them to go on. And they were snuffed out. Without premonition. Without last words. Their last thoughts cut short before a nerve-impulse could tell them to duck. Before they could finish their prayers. What sort of luck is that? Where was the glory in any of that?

I woke as the ambulance bounced over a speed bump. In the dark outside I could hear the rusty squeak of an opening gate. The ambulance came to a stop and the rear doors were opened. I struggled to my feet and limped toward a lit opening. Behind me I heard another vehicle slide to a stop and its own doors swing open toward me. I carried my boot in one hand, the chart in the other. I handed the chart to a man. "Whoa," he joked, "we got a walk-in?"

I attempted a smile but knew that the man found none in my expression. He ushered me through the door and made his way to the casualties stumbling or being stretchered in behind me. The medics inside recognized me immediately for who I was. "Where are you from?" was asked of me before anything of my injuries. I answered and was laid down on a stretcher at the far end of the room. One of the medics leaning over me had gotten ahold of my chart. "Texas, huh? How the hell did you wind up here?"

"I got shot," I answered.

The medic chuckled. "Fair enough. Can you tell me where?"

I pointed to the various locations where metal had pierced flesh on my body.

"Is this shrapnel or bullets?"

"Well I think it's only one bullet, but in a lot of pieces." I could hear a man on the other end of the room screaming, the medics were rushing to and fro, grabbing saline bags, punching IVs into arms. "It came through a wall. So I guess I was shot once, but it was all the fun of being shot five times." I was laughing now.

"What's your pain level like?"

I told them. They attached a syringe to my IV, and I watched as the medic depressed a plunger. "This is ketamine. So in about thirty seconds you're going to feel a little... *weird.* Don't panic, some people do, it's just so we can move you around without hurting you." I could hardly hear him over the screaming, the ringing in my ears, the pounding of my leg, the circling jets. Then it all went quiet.

It was as though I was having an out-of-body experience within my own body. I could see them turning me about. I was aware that they were prodding me, measuring me—this must have been what being abducted by aliens was like. But they were speaking English, sweet English. The screaming from the other end of the room was quiet now. That man's conscience must have retreated to the same safe corner inside himself that mine had. They removed my keffiyeh. They opened my shirt, took off my pants, piled my things on a shelf somewhere out of view. I lay naked before them. After a time, they covered me with a space blanket and then pumped me full of another dose of ketamine.

A man was now standing over me. He was waving like he was saying "Hello." He wore a black t-shirt with ARMY printed bright and bold and yellow across the chest. Lazily, my eyes looked up to meet his. His face was a silhouette against the bright lights in the ceiling. "Azad," he said. "Now, I know this is a bad time, but I have to ask you a very important question." Sweet English. "You've got a decision to make. Either you can go back with the YPG, the SDF–go through their medical channels, whatever that entails. You'll leave here and we'll have no record of you." And I knew this was coming. "Or, you can give me your information–your legal information as an American citizen and we can get you on a flight to Baghdad tonight, and you'll be going home."

I stared at him like a cow before I spoke, my inner self screaming out from behind dull eyes, "You picked a *bad* fucking time to ask me that, man. I'm high as shit."

The man cocked a grin at me. "I'm sorry buddy. I know. Now, you've got some time–a little bit of time. The decision doesn't have to be made right now, but it has to be made soon."

He had very little other information to give me. I would be on a flight to Baghdad. That was it. The logistics and ramifications of what was to come were as unknown to him as they were to me. I would have to decide to find out.

After a while, the room had cleared. It was cold. I was hungry. Jason, a man younger than I was, sat on a gurney next to me. I was still coming down off my high, and I could feel tears welling in my eyes.

"If it were me," Jason said, "I would go home through American channels. But I don't know what your situation is. I don't know how the SDF operates. I do know that if you come with us we can guarantee that you get home safely, we can make sure that those wounds heal properly–cleanly. Look at it this way, you're out of the fight. It'll be a month or two before you recover. And in that time you're recovering, we may be pulling out of Syria. Once we're gone, who knows what happens."

"Turkey invades," I said. Turkish President Erdoğan had been sabre rattling for months. How he would relish in the destruction of our revolution. How he would "bury us in our ditches when the time came." In the north of the country, unfriendly drones had begun circling–waiting for a moment to strike and set the whole thing off–to kill every Kurd in existence for the sake of Turkish nationalism. If there was any nation vile and brazen enough to wage a genocidal war in plain view of the world in today's modern age of communication and oversight, Turkey was the one. They'd imprisoned their journalists and their educators for speaking out against the regime. They'd invaded Kurdish-controlled Afrin with little pretext, and the world remained silent on the atrocities committed there–female fighters' breasts had been cut off of their lifeless corpses, YPG and YPJ hanged from cranes. Turkey had given ISIS fighters medical care when they were wounded, welcomed them with open arms to hospitals in Diyarbakir, where they were treated and sent back to the front. They'd funneled foreign ISIS fighters into Syria to fight against the Kurdish militias, and they'd recruited them to their Turkish-backed FSA ranks when they'd been defeated. ISIS, in the form of the FSA, was the acting Turkish invasion force, now backed by aircraft. It is comparatively easy to win a war when you control the skies and your enemy must live in constant fear of warplanes. The US could pull out any day and the enemy, their jets and drones, would be upon us–circling–striking.

Getting home was no certainty. And here the Americans were guaranteeing that much. And they were speaking sweet English. I wiped my eyes. I told him I would go back with the US Army.

I would have given my life gladly to the Kurdish cause and the Rojava Revolution—in defense of that land, and here I felt I had turned my back on them. The Americans began to drop their standoffish approach to me once I'd agreed to their help, they asked about my life, they brought me food and a blanket. But I was nothing more than an outlier to cut through their boredom. They wandered into the operating room where I lay in the corner, some spoke to me. Many gawked openly at my dirty face, my punctured uniform, the Kurdish scarf I had draped over my head and shoulders like a shawl.

The general of the frontline units of the SDF came to me late that night. "Dem baş, heval," he said. The medics offered to fetch me a translator. I told them I didn't need one. They hovered around like bodyguards, as though they expected to have to fight him off. I spoke to General Çîya for some time. He asked about my experience in Rojava, how I had been wounded, what I would do when I returned to my home country. I answered his questions in the best Kurdish I could muster. "Do you make this decision free of oppression?" he asked me. "They do not force you?"

"Yes," I said, a small reservation in my mind, a small seed of guilt. "Erê."

Çîya touched his forehead and his heart in a sign of compassion. He ripped the patches off his uniform and handed them to me. "Ser çavan, heval. Serkeftin." He shook my hand, turned, and left.

"Serkeftin," I answered. *Victory.* And though it did not seem like it alone in that hospital room—bandaged, bleeding—victory was close at hand. Daesh—ISIS—was on its last leg; only the night before, we had made the single largest advance in one night of the entire Deir ez-Zor Campaign. American airstrikes were crushing the walls and the wills of the remaining Islamic State fighters. Their weapons caches were being seized. International Daesh were being captured. Flags were falling. The SDF had swept through the suburban villages on the southern outskirts of Hajin, meeting little resistance. In Ash Sha'fah that day, ISIS launched what would be one of their final counterattacks of the conflict. I would bleed, 23 others would die. And the war would be over in 77 days. And victory would be declared and celebrated across the globe, the human cost of defeating the Islamic State largely unnoticed by those singing so loudly of its end. And here I was in the hospital room, cold.

"We weren't able to get you manifested to Baghdad tonight," the medic told me. "Probably tomorrow."

That was fine with me. I slept.

And I woke the next day and was brought Pop-Tarts for breakfast and warm bland food for lunch and supper. I read a book and sent messages relaying the situation to my friends still at the frontline and to my friends at home. More people popped their heads in when there were no patients being treated, like I was some sort of dirty zoo animal. Some asked me my name. "Azad," I told them.

"No, I don't mean your terrorist name," he replied.

Terrorist name? Were we not on the same side?

The following day, I still had not left. "We're still working on it," they told me. My foot had swollen up, and pain was lancing through my body. The medics told me that I needed to walk around as best I could to keep blood circulating in my leg in order to keep the swelling down. Not being a medical professional myself, I considered this sound advice. So I wandered, sporadically stumbling up and down the hallway, out into the cool desert air, and back inside again for a while.

"You can't be here," he spat.

I looked at him. His boots were clean. His shirt was freshly washed, and he sported the thick "tactical" beard so often seen borne by Navy SEALs in movies and disgruntled Iraq War Veterans wearing too-tight t-shirts. He was a sergeant.

"Why?" I asked.

In the brief instant before he spoke, I could almost see his brain going haywire as it tried to compute my response. Sparking, smoking like a cartoon. Someone had *questioned* him? "Because I fucking said so, and because this is *my* camp. And *you* can't be here –"

"Alright, calm down you fucking fobbit."

That got him going.

I cut him off again. "Look, Sergeant never-been-outside-the-wire 'MyCamp' I want to get the fuck out of here just as bad as you want me out, but the medic, who outranks you, told me I needed to walk around. So, you can take it up with him if you've got a problem with it."

He was so dumbfounded that I could see his jaw hanging open as I limped past him. It was the single moment in my life where the perfect thing to say and my spoken words lined up with one another.

Shortly thereafter I was told I could no longer leave the room without an escort.

In the hospital room I saw many patients–many of my comrades–come and go. Some were quiet. Others screamed in agony, writhing around violently, the tendons of severed limbs flapping about with gravity like pennants in the wind. The blood was dark. And they came. And they went, trio after trio. Some were maimed for life. Others, like me, would walk again and return to action or return to peace, but there was none among our number who would not be marred by that room every bit as much as we were marred by the battlefield forty miles south. Something is lost in the brightness of the eyes of every man and woman and child who has seen war and been unfortunate enough to walk away from it. It is a heavy burden. Brown eyes sink like mud. Green eyes curl over like grass in the summer. Blue eyes turn to ice.

"We're working on getting you out of here," the medic told me. I think we've got you manifested onto a flight to Erbil tomorrow."

"What happened to Baghdad?" I asked.

"We've been running into a lot of questions of legality with JAG and all that–you not having your passport, that kind of stuff."

I knew it could not have been as easy as it was made to seem while they were waiting on my decision. "Alright," I said.

I had been bent over and fucked by the Big Green Weenie of American military bureaucracy more than once in my life, enough to have a sense of what was to come. I hoped I was wrong. I spent the rest of the day lying there, reading. A major came and spoke to me. She gave me the number of an immigration lawyer. She told me to call him when I ran into trouble. I'd done nothing illegal, what good would it have done? No lawyers would be needed for anything.

The next day a pilot came into the room. "Are you Warren?" he asked.

I was. He shook my hand.

"We've got you manifested on a flight out of here this evening. I'll give you more information as we get closer to takeoff."

I would be leaving Syria by sundown, and home was close enough that I could smell the sharp winter air of Texas if I closed my eyes. The medic came into the room. "Did you talk to the pilot?" he asked.

"Yeah."

"Alright, well I've got a rundown of what's going to happen. We're going to fly you to Erbil, at the base there, we're going to look at your wounds and clean them again, make sure everything is doing alright."

"Ok."

"Then we're going to have to talk to the Iraqi government, and probably turn you over to authorities."

"What?"

He repeated himself. "Turns out we can't just stick you on a government flight out of there. We've got to play it by the book. They're saying you'd have to get a small interest-free loan from the federal government so that you can get a plane ticket home if you can't afford one yourself."

I stared at him in disbelief. "This isn't what I thought I was signing up for when I said I'd go back through American channels. That's not how it was made to sound."

"I know. I'm sorry. We can get you in touch with the US consulate in Erbil if you'd like. She might know more of the exact details."

"Yeah. Do that."

A while later, they called me into a small office criss-crossed by phone lines and ethernet cables. The walls were stacked from floor to ceiling with computers, blinking red and green lights. Three glasses-wearing men filed out as I was led in and handed the phone. "Hello?"

"Hi, this is Janie Springfield at the US consulate in Erbil. How are you doing today?"

"Good. I'm just wondering how this whole thing is gonna work."

"Ok, well they'll fly you in here, the Army will take care of your wounds. Then they'll get you here to the consulate. From there we have to go about getting you an emergency passport and dealing with the Iraqi authorities. Once they've got all of the information they need, we will hand you over to them. And you'll probably be detained."

"I'm going to jail?"

"Yes," she said in a preparatory way to where one knows that there is a "but" coming, and there are no "yes, buts" when it comes to going to jail; jail is jail, even a really nice one, and this one would not be one of those. "But they'll take very good care of you, and we here at the consulate will be coming to check on you every day, making sure that they're taking care of your wounds and everything. And you'll only be there for about a week, maybe a little longer. The Iraqi government will have you pay off a fine of 19 dollars for each day you overstayed your visa and then you'll be free to go. Then you find a place to stay and get a plane ticket and you'll be home in two weeks' time I'd bet."

The way she said all this was as though she were reading off a travel brochure to the finest resort in Nassau. "So you're telling me that you're going to throw me in jail with ISIS fighters—with the guys who just fucking shot me? And then I'm going to have to come up with 4,000 dollars to pay my visa fine after I've spent a week in jail?"

"There aren't former ISIS in these jails, it's mostly just petty criminals—people arrested for shoplifting. Stuff like that."

"No," I said. "No it's not. My friends were arrested crossing back into Iraq in November. They were jailed with former ISIS fighters and then the KDP threatened to turn them over to Turkish MIT."

"No," she said. "We will make sure you get home safely. They won't hand you over to Turkey. Think of the alternatives. Think of how dangerous it is to cross the border illegally. I don't want to be the one responsible for getting your body back to the United States. Now you weigh the options: a week in jail and the cost of the fees and plane ticket versus your *life*."

"Wait, I'd have to pay for the plane ticket too? What happened to the no-interest government loan?"

She paused for a moment, "The consulate doesn't do that, sir."

I turned towards the medic and his superior officer, both huddled in the corner of the tight little room. I shot them a glance of distrust. "So I'll fly to Erbil, get cleaned up, spend seven days in jail with former ISIS, then be on the hook for something like 7,000 dollars? Yeah, I'll take my chances with the SDF," I said into the receiver. "Have a good day." I hung up the phone and turned to the men in the corner. "I'm going back with the SDF. I'm not going to jail for this."

They led me from the room and back to my bed. They looked at me with the disappointment a parent might give a child who has an unshakable drug addiction that will one day kill them. "I'm going back with the SDF," I said. The medic turned and walked from the room, his head hanging heavy with contempt. His superior officer stood with his arms crossed.

"How do you know they'll take you back?" the superior asked me.

"They'll take me back." The Syrian Democratic Forces practiced a long-forgotten American tradition of loyalty. Those who fought for them, with them, would always be allies. Their backs would never turn to them. They would always be there for one another, for those that were there for them, even those that may have wavered in their confidence a little. A Kurd needs every friend he can get.

"Well," the officer said. "We'll have to see if you're in our *custody* or in our *care*."

I wanted to kill him. I wanted to take my crutch and bash his fucking face in. "I've done nothing illegal," I said. "I've done nothing against the law—nothing you can detain me for."

"We'll let JAG see about that."

"Get General Çîya. I'm not one of your men, and I'm going back with the SDF. I appreciate that you're trying to help me get home safe, but I will not be pinned to that cross because of your bureaucratic bullshit."

"Me, I don't give two shits what we do with you," he snapped. "For all I care you could take that flight to Erbil in thirty minutes, you could go back with the SDF, or we could turn you loose outside the front gate with a little bit of food and water and send you on your merry way. But I do things by the book. That's how I got my job, that's how I'll keep it." Then the officer turned and left. I could have run. I could have crutched my way across the base and to freedom, hobbling along with my belongings stuffed into a pillowcase and hitchhiked my way north to my YPG unit, but I sat in the cold and empty room and waited for the door to swing open again. "You're free to go," he said. "Çîya is waiting."

Çîya hugged me when we met again. "Come," he said in Kurdish. He led me across the large, white-walled building to a small room. "Wait here." And I waited, and the Kurds in the room offered me tea and sugar. Before long I was swept up by a new man. I followed him out the door into a cold Syrian night, the sky thick with stars hanging above a thin scattering of streetlamps on the Kurdish side of Green Village. It was quiet. There were no jets circling.

We walked a ways through a dense garden, down sidewalks canopied by the boughs of trees. We came upon an apartment complex. I was beckoned inside. "Welcome," a man said, a smile on his worn, wrinkled face.

"I will come back tomorrow," the man who was leading me said, and then he left

"Have you eaten?" the old man asked in Kurdish.

"Na," I replied. No.

He went into the kitchen and made a tray of fruit for me, placed it in front of me, and he disappeared out the door. I sat alone on a thick pad on the carpeted floor. Posters of martyrs hung on the walls. There was a diesel heater in the center of the room, its black cylinder warming the space comfortably. Fire burned inside. I was lost in it for a while.

Before long, the man came back, his arms were laden with plates of chicken and vegetables, rice, tomatoes, soup, and nan. He set the tray down before me. "Eat," he said. And I ate.

After the meal was finished and I leaned back against the wall, he offered me a cigarette. I took it and lit it and looked up towards the ceiling, watching the smoke rise. "What happened?" he asked.

I looked back at the man, our eyes met. And he was there with me in the dank darkness of the house. He too heard the mortars booming outside the building, felt the dust showering down from the ceiling, heard my radio crackling. "There's a sniper that's got us pinned down," came the voice of another westerner. "Copy." I said into the radio. I relayed the information and leaned my head back against the wall. The mattress below me was thick and comfortable. My rifle lay across my lap. Then he too heard the sharp rattle of machine gun fire. The men all around locked eyes and rose from lying or sitting. He grabbed his rifle with us. He too ran up the stairs once, a turn, and out into the bright January sun. He stared down the same sights of my same rifle and felt the recoil in his shoulder as in mine. He watched the enemy run. He fired as I fired. He felt the recoil in his shoulder as in mine. He too could feel the earth tremble, the mortars bursting around me. Rifles firing. The anger, white and hot. The sun, bright and cold above him as well. He too was there with me. He too fired his weapon and fired his weapon. And the wall burst. The bullet punched through it, shattered and hit him too. He felt the lurch of recognition, saw the blood thick on his uniform, his hands.

"Daesh sniper," I said.

He said nothing. He nodded. He handed me a cup of tea.

6 January 2019: Ash Sha'fah, Syria:

We slept briefly & left some time around midnight. On the shoulders of a Humvee, under the dull glow of flare lights, the 6 of us rode in breathless silence as we advanced nearly 3 kilometers to the outskirts of Ash Sha'fah. We stopped near a scrapyard & unloaded to the roof of a tall building. There we joked that Daesh must be finished—too scared to fight back as we rolled over what was left of their Caliphate.

"This must be how the Huns & Mongols felt!" - Berxwedan, atop the newly taken position.

Aşîtî & I were told to move over to the building next door. In the pitch black of night. Through a scrapyard. In mine-infested territory. But we did it in fear, & when we got there, we found Sîpong & the tabûr that we had left earlier in the day. Sîpong greeted us warmly in Kurdish & gave us a thick, warm blanket. I set it down on top of my things, & as Aşîtî & I were looking for a suitable spot to sleep on the roof it was stolen by one of the Arabs, who I found curled up with it on a thick sleeping pad. Aşîtî & I tried to get some sleep spooned together beneath paper-thin sheets in the cold of night. Just as I began to nod off there came a terrific sound like the sky was being ripped apart. A jet in its dive. Close. & then an even louder screeching tear & I opened my eyes to see a bright blinding flash zip across the night over me. I felt my heart contract with terror as the rocket made impact with the earth somewhere just on the other side of our building. Easily within 30 meters. Shrapnel & debris began to rain down on the rooftop. Half asleep, I covered myself with the blankets as I felt rocks raining down on me & felt a piece of shrapnel embed itself in my pillow. "Get to cover!" Aşîtî yelled, & I snapped to reality & rolled toward the wall. Once the air calmed & the dust all blew past us, we crawled back to bed, hearing Sîpong shout into the radio. I got no sleep in the frigid air that night. My eyes snapped open every time I heard a jet & more than once I rolled to the wall again in a panic. "Stop taking all the blankets," Aşîtî joked. He found some wood to burn sometime just before first light & the wind began to howl. In the morning, in the distance, in the city somewhere, a tire fire was lit & thick black smoke billowed toward us. "They are coming." The airstrikes stopped. I shot the wheels off a would-be VBIED parked in a garage nearby. Then the sandstorm started in earnest. First a Daesh mortar bombardment, then our own, shells all hitting around our 2 buildings. Aşîtî & Berxwedan went to the rear to find some water. Later, a sniper had Haqî & the others pinned down on the roof of their nokta across the car yard. We could hear the small-arms fire. 2 Arabs & I ran to the rooftop following the heavy-hitting sound of a DShK. I remember little of the fight. But I know at a point, I fired twice at two men. One two. & then the wall exploded by my face. "I'm hit," I radioed Haqî. & fucking stupid too. I was medevacked rearward. 2 SF Texans patched me up—an Aggie & a Sooner no less. Another of them went to a high school just down the road from my own. We ran track against each other. He gave me a pack of M&Ms. A 2-hour ride in the ambulance north to Green Village & the field surgery unit. Another Texan slapped his state flag patch on my chest & I made a ketamine-high decision to take a US military flight out of the country. Then fucking S—, who I hadn't seen in years, walked in the door. What a small world it is, even all the way out here.

10 January 2019: Green Village, Syria:

I wish I'd found that fucker. I should have looked high first & then low. I know I should have. I know I should have now. I hope I killed his friends. I know right where he must have been to have seen me. If only I'd just aimed there first. If only... The two shots fired at shadows running. & then the wall exploding by my face. More fear came from that, more came from the airstrike shrapnel than from the impact of the bullet. There was not even any pain—well, no exceptional pain. It felt like someone had thrown a rock at me, not even a hard throw. I bolted for the stairwell thinking it must have been a mortar, must have been a grenade—explosions were going off all around. I didn't find the wounds for a few minutes; only on the third pat down. A bullet hole in the back of the thigh. My prey turned predator. The flesh torn from the leg. Fragments in my foot, my armpit, cutting my cheek. A piece of me will always be in Ash Sha'fah—literally now, figuratively too. The man who should've been manning the Biksî at the kill hole beside me—who left me alone on the rooftop—tore a piece of cloth from his shirt sleeve & wrapped it around my leg—the white cotton dirty & grease stained—the bandage so loose that it immediately began to slide down my leg. I sat on the bed & radioed Haqî. He thought it was a joke at first. "Wait... hold on, are you wounded?" Then my training kicked in. I told Sîpong to radio for a medevac. I took my IFAK from my war belt & pulled the tourniquet from the pouch, wrapped it around my leg & twisted, applied a pressure bandage to the wound itself, & waited. The door opened & I was out it & back into brightness bristling with mortar bursts on the Biksî gunner's shoulders with explosions all around us. "Herre! Herre! Herre!" Go! Go! Go! You could hear the shrapnel whistling overhead. Then I was thrown in a Humvee & rearward. At the first stop, changing from the Humvee to a flat-bed truck, I saw our Tabûr Hilux parked in front of the post. I wanted to tell Aşîtî & Berxwedan where I was going, ask them to bring me my rifle, anything. "This is my car. My friends are here," I said in Kurdish. "Yes. They are, but you have to get in this car." "Will you tell them?" "Yes, only get in this car, you need a doctor." Rearward again until I was here. Here with these Americans who have never left the wire, who would not understand this or me, who do not care. If I wore a different uniform with a different flag on my sleeve, I would be lauded as a hero & have medals pinned to my chest. Instead I receive the incredulous stares one typically reserves for a 2-headed farm animal. Is a man's sacrifice any less meaningful because of the uniform he wears? Is your contribution to the world any more potent simply because you are an American? No. It cannot be. It cannot be. Every life holds itself as the most important. Each king's kingdom is the greatest. "If a clod be washed away by the sea, Europe is the less." Only those forces of evil, of hate, of genocidal & self-serving ambition are of a lesser station in life. & those who fight it, those who bleed from wounds seen & unseen, who suffer for the betterment of the world deserve the highest honor from those who would watch from the sidelines. You are not a child of the world until you make yourself. & the blood of a single martyr is worth more than the ink from the wells of a million cowards. The world is yours only if you are the world's. Fuck ISIS. Fuck terrorism.

& fuck Turkey. Fuck those who saw this plight & did not recognize it as their own. & damn those who turned a blind eye to Rojava. The ignorant have no excuse either. If you know what shade of lipstick Kylie Jenner is wearing on a Wednesday or how many passing yards Drew Brees has this season, then it is well within you to find something worth giving to this planet. The Rojava Revolution is a revolution for all humanity. None are of a higher order–be they American or French or Russian. Free people deserve a free life. I hope what I have given here has led to something. I hope I have left something remarkable. If I try now to go home with the Americans, they say I will spend at least a week in an Iraqi jail & be on the hook for something like 7,000 dollars I do not have. That about made the decision for me. I will try going back via YPG channels, which will hopefully work out well & quickly & not culminate in being airstruck to nothingness by Turkish drones. God-damned Green Weenie.

I left US care (or custody) & am back among the Kurds. What seemed like such a massive hurdle was in actuality nothing more than a short walk across the night. Many things are. I feel much more at home & welcome here. The food is better too (& free!). I should be heading back north tomorrow.

Something's Missing

Had you not survived this could you have become who you are? Did you mean to? No. It was all luck. You have made it through and now you must come to grips with it as others must accept the fact that they did not as they are falling... falling... falling.

But if you are honest with yourself–truly admit it, bright blinding flashes of anger and metal made you feel more alive than you ever did.

And then you are wounded.
And you claim to understand life.
And you are at home, at peace.
And it is dark.

15 January 2019: Noktaya Şehîd Kendal Breizh, Qereçox, Rojava:

I suppose I am still not sure I did not die there. I feel I am living a dream. It is good to be alive if I truly am. A good talk with Berxwedan today. He said going to fight a war as a young man ruined his life. He became trapped in this mode of revolution. Yet it was the greatest decision he ever made. It was the life he wanted to live. & this is the life I want to be living. He gave me some sage advice about going home. "Always have a goal," he said. Or else your life may become empty suffering. But my experience here is different from when he was my age. I feel I am still living in the interval of time between the wall bursting & the bullet's impact with my body. Trapped there, maybe. Over & over. But something ended there on that rooftop in Ash Sha'fah. Most of these days have been spent telling & writing of the front. How the hell do you impart all that to someone though? It is good to see my friends again. I spoke with the commander, & I should be headed home in 10 days. If all you have is 10 days & 10 days is your life... Nûbar, Haqî, & Aşîtî are still in Shaddadi. Somehow they lost the car in an ambush the day after I was shot. QSD took it for a medevac & (of course) promptly stole all the gear out of it. We managed to get the M-16 back, but all of my war trophies are gone & my sunglasses & the Biksî, the RPG, a Dragunov, grenades, ammo, the medical bag & who knows what else. Fucking QSD. At least we are all alright. Well, mostly alright. I am not the same person I once was. Mavros says I look 10 years older. I feel it too. Ash Sha'fah wounded me & Green Village ruined me. The front line was equally the most wonderful experience of my life & the most horrifying &

terrible. I do not know how to put it into words. I do not think it can be put into words. The actions can be described, what it was cannot. I guess I will spend my whole life trying.

23 January 2019: Başûr Kurdistan (Iraq):

Saying goodbye to my comrades may have been the hardest thing that I have ever done. We all promised to keep in touch as people always do, to visit one another, but it will never be the same. I cried. Brûsk & I went to the Academy & changed into our civilian clothes—ill-fitting after months without use. Our belongings were checked for any sensitive information, & we said our last goodbyes & then we left. We ate supper at the first nokta we had arrived at many months prior. It seemed foreboding & intimidating at the time, now it was only another base, another place out here. Mundane. Then the four of us—me, Brûsk, Kendal, & a man named Xelîl made for the border. "It's all over," I said to Brûsk just before boarding the boat at the Tigris. All over. All this is just a memory now, meant to collect cobwebs in one's mind until one day the dust is blown off to reminisce or blown off in horror & recoiled from. We loaded into trucks on the Iraqi side of the river & made a very uncomfortable ride into the mountains. We changed vehicles into a taxi under the moon beneath high, snow-covered cliffs & then continued on to Erbil. There we ate a lavish meal with the driver's family—dish upon dish upon final last dish of delicious Kurdish food, & then we bedded down for a few hours. Before dawn we woke & drove on to avoid the worst harassment of the security checkpoints. We had no trouble at any of them, luckily. We were never even asked for our passports. I slept most of the way, my wounded leg propped up over some bags in the third row of the taxi. & now we are again, at last, in the old safe house. It too feels mundane & of exaggerated importance. We've seen much more, much worse. They say we'll leave in the next few days; before the 26th, at least, & then go our separate ways. I hope we all have the same flight out. I hope we can get fucked up in Doha together—at least share a beer or a lucid conversation together again. I cannot believe it is over. I cannot. I survived the war. We survived the war. It feels stupid to say it, but my heart is full, & there is a strange kind of happiness about us all, covering the pain, the illness, the hurt & the sadness. The best times of my life were in Rojava. & I mean that, honestly. & if I am to be trapped, stuck, welded in my mind to one single moment, I am glad it is there in the sun on a dusty rooftop in Ash Sha'fah, the mortars hitting around me, feeling the recoil of my rifle forever in the infinity of time between when that wall burst & when that bullet hit, at the height of it all, in the center of the world.

Warren Stoddard II

An Serkeftin, An Serkeftin

Happy V-ISIS Day. Baghouz has fallen–that last shred of the Caliphate has been wiped away. Now you can boast proudly of victory.

In the fight against ISIS over 11,000 SDF fighters were killed, 45 internationals. They were men and women from Italy and Iceland, the UK, America, and many other nations. They are of little consequence. By their side fell 34,000 Iraqis, 8,000 Syrian Regime soldiers, 1,500 Peshmerga, 700 Egyptians, 101 soldiers from the Republic of Chad, 48 Nigerians, 35 Iranians, 71 Americans, 6 Cameroonians, 5 Turks, 9 Nigeriens, 3 Saudi Arabians, 93 Russians, a Canadian, 2 French, 3 Brits, and one Jordanian. They are of little consequence.

Over 14,000 civilians were tortured, executed, or otherwise killed by the Islamic State around the world. 7,000 or more women were abducted and sold into sex slavery. They are of little consequence.

More than 100,000 Daesh were killed over the course of the war. Nearly 12,000 citizens of Iraq and Syria were killed accidentally by Coalition airstrikes. They are of little consequence.

Over 10,000,000 people were displaced from their homes by the rise of the Caliphate. Ten million. They are of little consequence.

And so many others whose names we will never know and whose stories we will never hear because they were not entered into a spreadsheet nor written on the list of those people whose lives were left in tatters by the war. They matter not to us. We never knew them. They were not our family. They did not fly our flag. They are of little consequence. They lie dead and alone under rubble and stone.

"They could not believe it because they alone knew what their life meant to them, and so they neither understood nor believed that it could be taken from them." – Tolstoy: *War & Peace*.

And you thought it was only you.

Şehîd na mirin. Biji YPG.

Fuck ISIS.

-March 23, 2019

23 March 2021: Birmingham, Alabama, United States:

2 years on. What do you say here? That you can never outrun it? That you lie awake at night thinking of it? That even in comfort you relive it? The suck. That you were right when as a younger man you said the best times of your life were in a war? <u>*A war*</u>*. A war that still carries on. A war that has blossomed other wars that will blossom other wars still. A war that you tried to return to. & when you could not, it shattered you. You still long for war, to be amid the suffering. To ease it. You meant something there. Here you exist for Friday. Through a pandemic you curse that travel has been restricted & you cannot return to the war. Married to the love of your life & you long for the comfort of your comrades, the curves of a rifle, the grace of an artillery barrage. It is all photographs now; photographs & paragraphs on a page & flags in a trunk. As if the right alchemy of these things might bring it back, might place you among the shrapnel, might allow you to go home again. But you are always there anyway. The Tigris. The Euphrates. Hajin. Ash Sha'fah. Mind welded to a plain between two rivers. War never ends. War never ends. War never ends.*

Warren Stoddard II

When This Plane Lands

My god, he was drunk. But it didn't matter to the flight attendant. He finished one, and then with a raised index finger managed to order another without ever having to say a single slurred word to her. He turned to me sheepishly—a smile laced through with sadness, trying to forget our conversation. His eyes were half-closed. "Can you belieeeve they're still serving me?"

I chuckled lightly and turned back toward the window.

"You know, you've seen it," he said after a little while. "You've seen all of it, I'm sure. You've seen it." And his voice cracked—again. "I just—I just wish I hadn't, man. I didn't want to hurt them, those little *kids*, man. They were shooting at us; they were shooting at *our* birds. And *fuck you* motherfucker. I let 'em have it. I let 'em have it. You've seen it, I'm sure. Haven't you?"

I was silent. He'd asked me this question before. He'd asked it maybe a dozen times. I was unsure of what lie I'd told him. I didn't care to keep track any longer. I just nodded and took a sip of my drink. I could feel the wound on the back of my leg and the stiffness in my foot and the burning under my arm and the itching in my face and drank again to numb it away. I looked down at the liner of my jacket, checking to see if the hole was still there, making sure it had really happened—that there was tangible evidence of it because it was hard to believe any of all that now that I was surrounded by molded plastic and glass and drink menus and pretty women in stewardesses uniforms instead of that green-and-brown mixture of camouflage. And their hair was combed and brilliantly pinned back tight against their heads. They wore lipstick. I hadn't seen lipstick in a very long time.

"Man, Somalia fucked me up, man. And I am so fucked up. I'm sure you're fucked up too. You've been there, man. You've seen it, I'm sure."

I liked this man, this drunken buffoon sitting haphazardly in the seat beside me wearing a Muay-Thai fighter's uniform. I could not remember his name, but I was sure that I liked him if only for the simple reason that he was quite aware I was lying to him every time I answered one of his questions, and instead of saying anything about any of it, he simply seemed to glean the truth of any statement I made and carried on as if I had told the real truth all along. He took a final sip of another drink and ordered again with a raised index finger.

The flight attendant brought him one and I ordered another and sipped the fresh drink appreciatively and shifted uncomfortably in my seat. I wondered if I had bled through my pants or my shoes. The pants were dry, but the white shoe had a speck of bright red blood seeping from the inside. I took another sip of my drink and listened to the plane hum above the story of the man beside me.

This jet, I was sure, made the same horrific roar I had heard many times before not so long ago, that thundering boom and a shower of sparks and dust and concrete.

"You could see everything up there, man. We were just humming along over the top of these little square buildings in Mogadishu. People would look out their windows and duck back in. You'd see kids on the street corners hiding in the shade of the buildings, man. They'd run off and tell somebody else we were coming. But fuck, man, they could've heard us from a mile off. You know? US of fucking *A*, here we come, loud and proud, not exactly bashful. You know what I mean?"

I knew. I'd seen them, loud and proud and far to the rear of our fighting. They napped on couches in the sun, watching us take ground through binoculars, relaying our calls for air strikes. Trump had said they'd beaten ISIS—that America had beaten ISIS. Of course, to us they never seemed to be in any real danger at all—not in Syria anyhow. Hell, they thought we were out of our minds to be there.

"But man, over the summer there started to be more and more of those kids standing in the shadows on the street corner. More and more." He was staring intently into the television screen on the back of the head rest in front of him, but he wasn't paying it any attention.

I nodded in affirmation. I knew what was coming. I'd had that same stare this entire plane flight. I was sure I did. I could feel my eyes drying as they held open. I forced myself to blink, somehow snapping back from wherever far-off place I had been, growing further now as the minutes ticked and the engine hummed.

"And then they started shooting. Man, these *god-damned kids*, man. They stared shooting at us. And what the hell were we supposed to do? My CO hollered back to us 'Light 'em up!' So we did." He set his empty drink down and rubbed his eyes. "We lit 'em the fuck up. Holy shit. We lit 'em up. I was just holding down the trigger of my gun–I was a door gunner, you see? And I did my job. I did my fucking job... I mean, you know how it is. You've been there. You've seen all that fucked up shit."

I nodded again. I had seen the earth convulse violently and seen the shaky frame of the house we were defending vanish into the distance from the shoulder of an Arab man as shrapnel flew about. I had seen the enemy in the scope of my rifle. I had seen my wounds–simple enough to incite anger, painful enough to bleed red blood through the leg of my pants and my boot and my shirt and drip thinly through my mustache and eyebrow. I had seen the wall burst. I had seen the ceiling of the hospital, American faces and hands turning my limp body about. I had seen comrades come and go, some whimpering and clutching their stomachs, some bellowing and waving about the tendons of their severed legs. I had seen the black flag burned and cities razed. I had seen the sun rise and seen the sun set. But I had never seen a plane land.

"Those kids just fell like dominoes. And you could hear the rounds of their AKs hitting the body of the chopper. You could see them dying, drowning in their own blood, my tracers still carving them up. Shit, man." He began to cry.

I wondered if he did this with all fellow transcontinental passengers he found himself seated next to, or if I was one of a lucky few. I wondered if I would one day do the same.

"God. That shit fucked me up," he said after a while. "I don't guess I'll ever get over it, man. And you won't either. You won't." He looked me in the eyes as a kindred spirit, as a fawn might stare into those of a buck it sees off in the distance. I knew he was looking for some reassurance. I had none to offer. I was looking for it myself.

"What did you do when you got home?" I asked.

He blew hard through his nostrils and widened his eyes. "Drugs, man," he said and then guffawed. "A *lot* of drugs. I was fucked up on the streets for a while. No, not a while, for a long time. I got home in '94, didn't have a job till 2008 or so. Lost it, got caught in it all over again. Then I fuckin' found Muay-Thai. I love that shit, man. I go all around the world, just beating on people—loving them too. It gets my anger out, my sadness. I got a lot of both."

I looked toward the seat in front of me with that same faraway look in my eyes that he'd held in his. I hoped this wasn't what I had to look forward to.

"But you can't fall into that shit, man. I know you've seen the very same fucked up shit I have. Don't let it eat you up."

War corrodes everyone and in the aftermath there are many eaten so badly by the acid of it that they lose sight of themselves or jump back into the vat or succumb to those fresh, acid-born demons. Very few see the light in any of it—humanity is gone to all who have walked those steps and felt the sting of killing. Yet some deify it in the manner of Greek gods or Trojan horses, lauding its efficiency and beauty and craftsmanship, never mind those hells it holds or the corruption of the soul or the bodies of the children, the bodies of their mothers, the bodies of their fathers, the bodies of their elders, the bodies of their leaders, the bodies of their heroes fallen as Achilles fell shot through not the head or the heart but the ankle—not a life-preserving organ, but that in the extremities, that which moves you along, that which propels you forward—and unable to move forward and so trapped in the war, you die, you die, and you die—if not by bullets then by shrapnel and if not by shrapnel then heat and if not by heat then courage and if not by courage then cowardice and if not by cowardice then blind, foolish love for some great banner or cause and if not by love then by hate, hate of the enemy or hate of the self in the aftermath when the fire is gone and the bullets are gone and the heat and the songs and the arms and armor and friends and foes all fade away and it is only you alone in an ever-darkening room with the walls closing in about you as you pray, pray to god that something, any god of the machine, any deus ex-machina might come and save you miraculously or stoically or in any manner from your very self for it is the self in the end that kills you for the things that you have done and the jobs completed and the crimes committed if not against humanity then nature and if not nature then the self, for the self is the enemy and the enemy is the self no matter how different or divided they may have seemed from across no-man's land or on the other side of a hospital room or through the scope of your rifle, for you knew you could just as easily have been born them and they you, and instead of them it would be you lying there with the flies whirring about your face with arms leaden in death and though trying, unable to swat them away.

"It probably already has," I said, truthfully now.

"War is a sonofabitch," the man said, and he ordered another drink. "And coming home might be harder. You've got all those loved ones you ain't seen in ages, and that girl you haven't felt in months, and all those friends that want to take you out on the town and show you off like some sort of hero, but you know inside that you're just *gone*. You're not there at home, and you're not where you're always going to be in your head so *what the fuck is the point in any of it*?" He sipped his fresh drink, and then he turned to me and slurred dramatically. "Iwish I'd neverleft that fucking place totellyouthetruth, frien'. It was somuch easier to exist there. It's the leaving that gets you."

"Don't I know it."

"No telling what the fuck's bound to happen to you when this plane lands."

I nodded.

"They had no idea you were over there did they? The gov'ment?"

I shook my head.

"You might be *fucked*."

I nodded and laughed. "Might be."

"Well," he said, "at least you were doing the right thing. The Peshmerga is good people," he said.

And then he turned to me and I swear to god I could almost see him wink, as if he knew the truth of the lie I had told him. He most certainly probably did, but he said nothing of it.

"Yeah, I never been to Iraq," he said. "But I hear it's a pretty fucked up place."

"ISIS are some pretty fucked up people."

"Yeah, but it's over now, ain't that what Trump said?"

I wanted to tell him that President Trump had declared the defeat of the Islamic State precisely 20 days before I was shot on the front line fighting against them liberating a small Syrian city he had never heard of named Ash Sha'fah, but I did not. "Just about," I said. "Just about."

"Well," he said, "maybe they'll give you a medal or some shit."

"They'll probably just arrest me," I joked, and we laughed.

"Wish I still had my medals. I traded 'em for dope back when. Used 'em to get high. Didn't mean much to me then, but them scraps of ribbon was *something*, you know? Something to prove that at one time I'd been somebody... done something... something good... I hope, but I know...."

I nodded, and he said nothing more. When I looked over, he had slipped into a drunken sleep and soon I did the same.

And when I woke the Atlantic drastically, suddenly morphed into land of rolling green and high mountains. I looked at the landscape pass beneath the plane wishing that just maybe I could will it to be the Syrian plains or the Zagros Mountains or the deserts of Deir ez-Zor, but I could not. There would be the wheat fields of Kansas, not Jazira.

Mt. Washington, not Mt. Qereçox. This would not become Kurdistan or Northeast Syria. No green or yellow triangle pennants fluttered in the breeze, but instead the stars and stripes. This was America. I was home again. And home felt a very strange and foreboding place.

To see old friends felt a farce. I was not the man I had once been. I was not even a shell of him. I was something else entirely. Niha, navê min Azad e. Min jibo azadîya Kurdistanê şer kir, min birîndar bûm. Daiş dijminê min, dijminê Kurdistanê, dijminê hemû insanî ye. Min Daiş kuştin. Şoreşa Rojava jibo hemû insanî ye. Rojava welatê min e. Niha, ez Kurd im. What would they understand of that?None of it. If they had they would have been there beside me. Everyone would have, everyone should have, and I hated them for their silence. I will hate them forever in some small part for their silence. Backbreaking silence. Silence kills.

And in that moment for the first time I wished I would have died there. I had been living on a dusty rooftop in my mind for weeks now, and knew that I always would, so I wished that that had been the end of it. But I was stuck, stuck in the instantaneous interval of time between the wall bursting and that bullet shattering and hitting me five times over. But god, I wished that had been the end of it. No matter how sweet homecoming would be, no matter how good it would feel to again hold Noelle or share a beer with an old friend or any of those other pleasures of the first world, I wished that it had ended there on the front line, ended there at the pinnacle of everything, at the epicenter of that moment in the world. God, I wished I had died there.

How much trouble it could have saved me, but all those things I'd have missed....

The man beside me woke with a start as the plane landed. And I felt apprehension grow in my chest like a balloon squeezed tight in a vise. The people around us all stood and began to unload their luggage from the overhead bins. The man was still drunk. I could feel the warmth of my keffiyeh around my shoulders, and the torn liner of my jacket, and the warmth of the blood in my foot and the heat of aggressive pain in the back of my leg and I wished I had died there or changed my name forever to Azad and never thought of returning to the land I now sat in. I wished I had given my life for our Revolution and in defense of so much humanity and in striving for so much good in the world, but now I would have to make what I could of what I had left, or let the demons come for me and let the weight of it all consume me.

The intercom chirped and a peppy voice rang out over the speakers. The 400-some people standing and unloading their luggage from the bins looked up confused. "May I have your attention passengers; we need everyone to please retake their seats. We apologize for the inconvenience, but there is someone we need to remove from the plane."

There were confused mutters and annoyance tittering in the background. The drunken man beside me and I looked at each other and smiled. He reached across the empty seat between us and slapped playfully at my chest. He spread a broad grin. "They're coming to get your ass!" he said happily.

And they did.

Acknowledgements

Several of the works contained in this volume were originally noticed and appreciated by print publications around the world:

"Ghanima" first appeared in the Spring 2020 issue of *As You Were: The Military Review*, a project by the American nonprofit, Military Experience & the Arts.

"A Return Home" first appeared in the September 2020 issue of *Samfiftyfour*, a globally collaborative literary magazine.

"A Good Place on the Banks of the Euphrates" first appeared in the Spring 2019 issue of *Persona Literary Magazine*, a publication of the English department at Texas State University.

The photograph "Airstrike in Ash Sha'fah" first appeared in the February 16, 2019 edition of the *New York Times.*

"Through All That Angry Air" first appeared in the Spring 2020 issue of the *Barely South Review*, a publication of the MFA program at Old Dominion University.

"As All Wars Do" first appeared in the April 2020 issue of the Norwegian literary magazine, *Griffel.*

"Something's Missing" also first appeared in the Spring 2020 issue of *As You Were: The Military Review*.

"When This Plane Lands" first appeared in the Fall 2020 issue of the Canadian literary magazine, *Into the Void.*

Three of this volume's stories: "Into the Sun, Alone," "Or the Lack of It," and "Marienplatz" were written during my time in Rojava between training exercises, language classes, and operations. Their themes on leaving home and returning from war reflect mine and other international volunteers' daily conversations together while in Northeastern Syria. Without that hevaltî, none of us would have made it.

A special thanks goes to my mother for her help in editing this text, and an apology for the worry war caused her.

Global gratitude is owed to the native sons and daughters of Albania, Argentina, Australia, Canada, Egypt, France, Germany, Iceland, Iran, Italy, the Netherlands, Portugal, Slovenia, Spain, Turkey, the United Kingdom, and the United States who gave their lives as members of the international units of the Syrian Democratic Forces in the war against ISIS and to the more than 11,000 Syrian Kurds and Arabs they fell beside. Şehîd na mirin.

About the Author

Born in 1994 and raised in the Hill Country of Central Texas, Warren Stoddard II attended Texas State University in San Marcos, where he majored in English. Following his graduation from Texas State, he traveled to Syria to join the YPG, a Kurdish militia, and was later wounded in action liberating the city of Ash Sha'fah from ISIS control. Upon his return to the United States, he moved to Birmingham, Alabama, where he married Noelle, was a member of the Chopper Kai Dojo, and rode his Harley across America.

His short literary work has been featured in *Dice Magazine*, *The Renegade Conflict Journal*, *Beyond Words Literary Magazine*, and numerous other publications. He is also the author of *No Birds in Yesterday*, a novella.

warrenstoddard.com

www.ingramcontent.com/pod-product-compliance
Lightning Source LLC
Chambersburg PA
CBHW030739110726
47900CB00008B/2378

* 9 7 8 0 5 7 8 9 6 4 8 4 3 *